One Man Three Women

Peter Jorgensen

September

Wednesday 1st September, 2010

Surrounded by Girls at the Age of Ten

Normally I do not need an apology or an explanation to grant myself a glass of cognac, but on this first night of the autumn, I can think of several reasons to enjoy the dark-golden alcohol.

Firstly, as noted, it is now autumn. Secondly, I have just received an email from Elizabeth in which she good-naturedly teases me for my tardiness. And that means my third excuse is the need for a good deal of thinking during the coming hour. It was fun to bump into Elizabeth back in May, when we met at a brunch seminar covering the future of gender roles where men and women create the future together. And when I found out that Elizabeth – to the surprise for some people and dismay to others – had managed to live her life according to the model with three men, I was tempted to self-test the model but with three women. The idea has grown since, and with Elizabeth's email I realize there might be a deeper reason I find the idea so appealing to me.

Back in 1972 when I was 10 years old, my family was stationed for 18 months in Brazil. Our good and safe, traditional family was subjected to a bit of a cultural experience, and the first challenge was to find an apartment. After we were shown around by a broker and found a small and cozy complex suitable for our needs, my parents abruptly got a message from the broker's boss that it was not possible for a family with a boy kid of 10 to rent the place. My older sister was not a problem, but their experience with boys was bad. Thus, all other tenants were either childless or had daughters only. My parents discussed their options. Should we go find a new place, or would my

4

parents send me away to boarding school? Fortunately not. My parents persuaded the boss to let us stay a month to begin with by promising to replace any vandalism and keep a tight leash on me. I thought no further about this droll fact back then. I did not realize it meant that I would be surrounded by girls.

The months passed and I behaved myself properly. Being around all the girls of different ages opened my eyes to how different girls are. First and foremost by nationality, and it has certainly played a role in relation to the first four years in an ordinary Danish primary school in the seventies, where most kids were quite similar. Possibly it played a role as well that I, as the only boy among all the girls – and being a blond Scandinavian – got quite some attention ...

In the great mix of exciting cultures, it became obvious to me at a relatively young age what a wonderful variation one can find among the opposite sex. As in the classic child's game where you flip through a catalog full of toys, I could not decide which one of the girls, I liked best. There was the exotic type I just found indescribably attractive. There was the confidential type, with whom even a young boy could imagine spending many years and being a wonderful partner – and as I was thinking, why settle for two? I also liked the fresh and slightly wild-at-heart type, with whom it was fun to play and compete, but I set the limit at three in order to keep track.

Even back then, all three types were represented in my life, but I was too young and shy to get serious about anything.

With that background, it may not be so surprising that Elizabeth's model appeals to me. It's now been some years since my complex and ultimately wrecked marriage, so it's time to get back in gear. Tomorrow I will create a profile on the same dating site Elizabeth used and start my search for three women – maybe I can get back at the wild type of woman and the exotic woman.

Thursday 2nd September, 2010

Club30

Just as I was about to create my online dating profile, I received a text message from my friend, Robert: "Come share a Barolo with me!"

I don't see Robert very frequently, although he recently moved into a cozy house just three streets away from my penthouse in Copenhagen. Robert has always radiated a self-confidence about the size of Kilimanjaro, he is extremely generous and a good father to his two children. As in so many other cases they are now part-time children, and his son will soon be moving out. His daughter is still in school and both kids seem very balanced, which I attribute to Robert's abilities as a loving and comforting father, despite the divorce some years back. Robert has never concealed the fact that he is a member of the so-called Club30. The first time I heard about this concept, I was a little disoriented. It's about always having a girlfriend who has not yet turned forty.

- Hey Chris, come on in. With a big hug and a bottle of good red wine in hand, he showed me to the couch. His living room is sparsely furnished with a sofa and two leather armchairs, a beautiful carpet under the coffee table adds to the coziness, and his place is always immaculately clean. With a job paying extremely well, Robert is in a position to hire household help.

- What's up, you're all by yourself tonight? I asked.

- Yes, sonny boy is on a night shift and the chick is with her mother. And, hmm ... Tina, well she, hmm, we are not seeing each other quite as often right now.

Robert and Tina had been practicing the modern "Living-Apart-Together" philosophy for the past few years. She has her own house and lives there every second week, and every other second week with Robert. Or at least that's how things used to work.

- On a break again? I asked.

- Yes, EXACTLY! That is precisely the case! Robert exclaimed – rather too loudly. But with his mischievous smile, I could see that he right there and then had found his option. That he might not have been abandoned, but simply was in his fourth or fifth break in the relation with Tina.

- How many breaks have you actually been through, and why now?

- I found out that I stopped missing her during the weeks when she was not here. So I had to draw my conclusion and react. I told her that she deserves better. She needs to have a boyfriend who respects her.

- Oh no, Robbie, you can not put it on her like that! As if it's to her advantage that you have run out of steam ... That is not fair.

- She is approaching the age limit, too. You know, I have my principles.

During the last half of the excellent Barolo we got no closer to a solution to Robert's dilemma. My plan to mention the idea of a dating profile was discarded. It seemed like poor timing, and I already know his reaction, I'm pretty sure. On several occasions he has urged me to use network dating and is convinced that I would get lots of inquiries. However, the new plan is somewhat different. But there's a time and place for everything. Sometimes I also have to be there for a good friend who is in need for a little talk. It's not that the talk has been wasted for me. Finally, here was a couple who practically lived together, but separately. I would have thought it worked out. As long as both I and they ignored the age limit. But even this model is no guarantee that things work out, it seems.

It therefore means that my own internal reflection has a new twist. Do I put in my profile, which I will create tomorrow, that I openly search for three different women? Yes – better be open about it. They have a right to know what they are getting into. Elizabeth was honest as well when she posted her profile, so she will taunt me if I'm not. My wording might suggest that my childhood difficulty at choosing still affects me as an adult. I wonder if there will be several to choose from, if I write that I'm not picky?

Ha! Not picky. Not true at all. It will be an interesting challenge to phrase the profile text tomorrow evening.

Friday 3rd September, 2010

In Search of Three Women

The day began like any other working day: I jogged six kilometers around the lakes before I cycled to my shared office space downtown. We are a group of independent specialists in various areas of IT, communications and digital media, and we all benefit from each others' skills. It fits me nicely being my own boss, and I appreciate the freedom to work only when it suits me. Also to be able to work from home but be online with collaborators in all parts of the world when projects allow.

But tonight is all about something else. I will create an online profile that can help in finding three new women in my life. And Elizabeth has set something in motion for me with the model. She has been a catalyst for something that has remained and been simmering in my subconscious ever since childhood. One woman is not enough.

So, I must define my three wishes. The three types of women. I have to articulate it, so I discourage fewest possible candidates. I must be honest. It should be a profile with photos, because I myself would only want to answer queries having one or more images. The profile text should also explain that I search in an area fairly close to Copenhagen. Including the outskirts of Denmark requires more than common love, and finding a place to date could also be a logistical problem, although I own a motorbike. Honestly: Would I bother to meet in Svendborg, for example, even with a very exciting woman to whom I'd been exchanging a couple of emails? Don't think so.

Well then. Photo and area. It's almost like being a realtor, but without the cliché-filled and fancy descriptions. It is simply too ridiculous and makes me think of an old advertisement for multimedia technology. "Yes, I'm sort of Latino" – hey, send a picture, honey!

During my search on the internal and several external hard drives for images, I could put on my online profile, it dawns on me that most photos are from vacations made in recent years. Contrary to expectations, as we have all advanced from celluloid and paying through the nose for prints, my numerous digital cameras have not left myself with many visual memories – at least not with myself as a motive. To start a home photo session seems a little absurd, so I must choose some shots from my archives. It is probably not wise to show too much skin, in other words, yours truly in swimming trunks, and the dating site might not allow it, either. A couple of portraits is probably okay? But I'm obviously wearing sunglasses in most cases. Does it really have to be so difficult? And I've not even started to describe my desired dates. What a hassle.

In an attempt to put aside vanity for awhile, I decide to describe the women I would like to hear from ...

Dear future woman in my life. You can identify with one or more of my wishes for the perfect (no, had better change that to suitable) ... The suitable partner, which, as I, find balance in yourself, but also lack somebody to share the good life with.
I realized early on that my greatest challenge is the difficulty of choosing, and that's why you must also be ready for me to have several women in my life. That may be a bit of a challenge, but I can promise you full attention when we are

together. Similarly, I can promise you that you will never be exposed to jealousy on my part – I'm fair that way. I am honest, and because I openly declare my potential need for several types of women in my life, this also means that I accept the same attitude on your part. If you are single and seeing others, it's OK. If you are in a relationship, but need a little extra spice, it's OK. I will never own you and you never will own me. Our relationship must be based on a mutual desire and a mutual understanding of these rules.

Gosh, what am I doing? Will there really be women out there who reflect on such an opening? On the other hand, what have I got to lose? And, if Elizabeth could find her three men, then I can find my three women!

On with the text.

Now, in order to define somewhat more precisely what I'm looking for, I will tell you about the types of women who are sure to get answers to their queries.

One of the three qualities – or types that I search for is The Exotic:
You are exotic, both in appearance (yes, I'm visually oriented like most men) as of mind. You can do very impulsive things and you're probably either of foreign origin or have southern blood in years. And I am not talking about the south of Denmark here, but decidedly and truly latino. You are aware of your feminine benefits, and you use them fully. When I walk on the streets with you, I would be delighted to see all the other men wringing their necks to enjoy the sight of your swinging hips, and it is your very natural walk. I know that you are aware of this quality, and together we will enjoy that you are with a man who desires

you for your specific innate genes. Because you bring forth the proud hunter in me – look, I have captured the best specimen. And in our shared joy, we find purpose, because you are delighted in the certainty of sharing your life with the guy, who was man enough to grab you – unlike all the others who get anxious around your beauty. When you least expect it, I come up with the strangest ideas, and you need the opponent. One day I plan a trip or prepare a great dinner, when you thought it was just a regular day in our lives. And because you are so open to new approaches and unplanned events, such impulses would be entirely consistent with your personality. You cannot live without this and I cannot live without you. We are both aware that we are on loan and our common strength of the relationship is that we choose each other – as long as we do. And the longer we do it, the stronger our bond.

The second quality – or type – My Soulmate:
You are the epitome of comfort. I can entrust you everything, and vice versa. We are each other's best friend, each of us fills up the parts that our parents occupied in our upbringing. Not just to compare with our parents but also with siblings and friends up through puberty. We rely entirely on each other and as with parents, siblings and friends, we also know that there will always be others in our respective lives, which play an equally important role. Thus we only own one another when we are together. There has to be be room for others, and it is really a necessity for us to function. We are both aware that the other person has further meaningful relationships, but it's not a threat to what we have together. We can imagine ourselves being together when we are old. We may live to see that we are sitting on a porch and drink tea or gin-tonic, while we watch the sunset. Our lives are meant to grow old together because we are

soul mates. Because we have this built-in security, it means nothing that we both have others in our lives - although it sometimes involves deeper conversations with others, very different experiences with others and even sex with others. How can that be done, you may ask? And my answer is that it can be done, because nobody can be everything for another. Think about it, my possible future soul mate.

The third and last (because otherwise I lose track) – The fresh and slightly wild-at-heart woman:
You are aware that I'm only a temporary experience in your life. Thus, you are also young enough to regard our relationship as such: One more step forward, a joy that you will not miss out on. It goes without saying that we do not have long term plans, but we take the days as they come. I can guarantee that you will get experiences beyond your normal life and similarly I can get a wisp of surprises. Since you are probably somewhat younger than I, you are likely to contribute with a breath of freshness. You are looking for some form of security that I can provide, because I am mature and have mastered all the things your peers have never thought of yet. Been there, done that. I know where we should travel to get the best vacations. I know the best restaurants and not infrequently their owners. You will be treated as a princess and have many experiences to remember me by if we do not – to our mutual surprise – choose to continue our lives together. We may, after all, both find the peace we are looking for in the middle of all that impulsivity this constellation makes room for?
But, as initially said: I am ready for you to enter a relationship, knowing that you are chosen because you are young and we both know that our shared joy is not eternal.

All right, that describes my upcoming three women. There will hardly be any asserting that they qualify for all three, as Elizabeth experienced when she looked for her intellectual partner, her handyman and her lover. There is probably more risk of no response whatsoever. On the other hand, a good mantra is: Why not jump into it? Finally, I selected a few photos during the trawling of my hard disks, and they are fairly good, so in a few minutes I should click the button. I just need to re-read my text.

Yes, it is okay. That I did not get around to talking to Robert about this the other day does not matter much, because Ulrich is coming for dinner on Monday. I have known Ulrich since we were seven and eight years old, respectively. He is currently adjusting to life as being part-time-father after the world's longest attempt to save a marriage. We have been through many deep conversations over the years. We've even been through the problem that I was dating his ex-girlfriend in our late teenage years, which is probably the ultimate test of a friendship. As our friendship has survived, I can probably share my new plan with him. And I'm curious to hear his input. It's always exciting to hear other peoples' opinions – not just from women, though historically I have been dominated by female input, but when it comes to male choice and opportunity, there is nothing as good as a man-to-man talk. And Ulrich is probably my best bet for that. Sometimes he can spend a whole evening talking about his own problems, but that is a part of the deal, and in his current situation, I certainly understand the need.

I hope Monday will be different so I can tell him about my own newly uploaded profile and expectations. It's too unlikely nothing will happen.

Monday 6th September, 2010

One Man and Two Women

It is probably with good reason that someone once came up with the saying that the joy of expectance is the greatest. It soon became apparent that my fears about Ulrich's need to talk were fully justified. Already as I was in the final stages of preparing dinner and we enjoyed time in the kitchen, I could sense where the conversation was heading.

- How are you coping with everything, now that Karen has finally moved out? I asked to initiate the status update.

- Ha, you would enjoy seeing what it has meant to the cleanliness at home. Neither the living room nor the kitchen is a mess anymore.

Ulrich has always been an organized guy, and I had often wondered how he and Karen with three children could live in an eternal chaos of everything from toys, clothes and old newspapers to pots and pans all over. Not that it was necessarily unhealthy, but I know Ulrich. Precisely this aspect has caused problems in their relationship but not enough to split up. He wanted the traditional family, probably more than Karen when it comes down to it. She was the one being unfaithful several times and already in the beginning I felt physical pain when seeing Ulrich's life crash.

- But how do you find time for everything? I mean full time job, part-time children, shop for food. I continued to give him the opportunity to unload his frustrations.

- Well, it's only every other week, I have the kids. And during the alternating weeks I scoot around quietly and clean a region at a time. I also have plans to fix the entire kitchen. New doors, varnish the floor, repaint the walls.

- Yes, sounds just like you. Handyman par excellence!

- The entire extra living room also has to be demolished and rebuilt. There is a problem with moisture in the ceiling.

- Are you insane? That's not something you can fix by yourself!

- Well, a few good friends and some beer, it will work out.

- I respect your optimism, but it takes more than a sledgehammer, and it may even become a little dangerous. But it is guaranteed to be one of the best forms of therapy after years of psychological warfare. Get your aggressions out like a cave man. If I have to participate, it will presumably be as a spectator.

- You can cook for us, said Ulrich and looked hungrily at the finished meal I carried into my dining room.

- Deal! There is actually something I want to discuss with you, I said as we sat down. I thought it would be good timing to speak, while Ulrich enjoyed the food.

- Do you remember Betina, I met at that seminar last month?

It seemed that he had not heard my last sentence.

- You know, the lady who is married and has two children and never wanted to leave her family.

- She was definitely a little crazy about you. And you probably don't even need to worry about Karen, now that you are separated?

- We ended up in her room, but we did not go to bed together. That is, we ended up sleeping, but we did not have sex.

- What? Now you confuse me. You told me that she was a catch.

- She still is and we flirt big time when we meet. But ... I don't know. It is as if I no longer get turned on in the same way as before.

- Thinking about Karen still?

- No, certainly not in that way. It was just different. I think we both had more need for closeness and the exciting opportunity. But we kept it to that when it finally became a real option.

- Hmm. OK, we are not in our twenties anymore. But you surprise me anyway.

Here was my best friend and he was telling me that he had had a chance for an adventure, we always during our adolescence had wondered about. Not necessarily containing a threatening divorce and related frustrations, but an affair just for the sake of lust - non-committal, playful and delicious, where both parties are aware in advance that it does not become more. The basic ingredients of good gymnastics! And then he said no! What's he doing? He was quiet a bit before he sadly continued.

- Sometimes I feel less as a man.

Oh, no. Ulrich is going down the slide ... I have to cheer him up!

- Pull yourself together. Think of the experience as a pleasant memory. And you say that you're still flirting. Don't you get a lot of fun from that? And your conscience is clear.

Again I become solution-oriented. Try to find the positive, to encourage and find new angles. Ulrich is quiet.

- You have always been a hit with the chicks. Athlete with a largely free access to all shelves. That Karen proved to be wrong for you is just bad luck.

- Easy for you to say. If she moves too far away, I am liable to lose the children.

- Is there any possibility of that?

- She has not decided yet but is looking for an apartment far away.

- Damn. Because her new boyfriend lives there?

- Yes, and I cannot do anything about it.

Defeat upon defeat. Perhaps I should have served Red Bull instead of beer, so the atmosphere was less like a funeral ...

What on earth could I do here? The vast majority of times I've seen Ulrich during his many years of crisis, he has been hopeful. Maybe because he thought they would save the marriage. That she despite extra marital affairs one day would fall back in the good family role. Now it's definite, and Ulrich knows. He will spend many months licking his wounds. I really hope for him that he could meet someone new.

- What about that Betina? Do you see her more often now?

- She has invited me on wellness weekend.

Suddenly he lights up with his boyish smile. Phew. Finally, a twist.

- That's great!

- Yes, but I would not want the kids find out. They are with Karen, and it is best if they did not know I'm seeing someone.

- Don't you think they would accept that you are actually able to continue with your life and be happy?

- It just seems wrong.

- Hm. I don't agree, but it's obviously your decision. I won't tell them.

Deep down I am completely convinced that it would make his children happy, both on his behalf and because they would have a happier father. Not necessarily a spare mother, and not at all right now, but still. There has been enough trouble and bad moods earlier. Is it really better to leave them in the belief that daddy is the abandoned one who devotes himself to half a home? Would they not approve if their father starts a new relationship or just gets a little happiness again?

- Maybe you should just focus on the near future. Luxury stay at a spa, tearing that room down and fix the kitchen. Hahah. You'll get busy!

We had managed to get the mood up again, and he helped with the dishes before he drove home. Difficult as it is to get acquainted with his situation, I sit here with a feeling that there is a heavy cloud resting over his life - hard pressed financially, without the opportunity to share his joy with the children. No one in the family with whom to share your everyday joy, which has always been his greatest wish. He would probably not have been able to give especially good input to my project for now.

Tuesday 7th September, 2010

The First Response

When I awoke this morning, I knew it was time to check whether there had been responses to my profile. But I postponed it a few hours and first put in a concentrated effort on a presentation I need for a client meeting next week. And because I worked at home today, I could take a couple of hours afterward to check up on replies to my online dating profile – great to be my own boss!

There were 14 responses! Not that this was overwhelming, but so much easier to take in. Always be positive, always curious and always patient. There is still time to get more inquiries.

In the user friendly interface I noticed that there was someone who had responded from a profile without photo. I have my principles about not answering those without a picture, but I read the relatively short message:

Hi Christian,
Funny ad – hope you can keep track if you get three such different women for sexual relations! I think Elizabeth got real busy when she put her ad up.
When I read about your three types, I am sure that I have soulmate potential. But I'm too naive about some of life's circumstances and need someone who can commit themselves. And I can be completely exotic on the right day, so for now I apply for all three. But for various reasons we need to start by email. Unfortunately I cannot give you a picture. But give me a little more substance. Who are you deep inside?
Love Lizzy

Whoah, a greedy woman who wants everything without giving anything back. That name is clearly an alias. Unless she has seen a numerologist.

Hi Lizzy,
The reason why I'm looking for three different women, is that I no longer believe in the existence of one and only one out there who can make me happy in the long run. And why go from one relationship to the next if we can extend the duration of several relationships to everyone's advantage? I am not speaking of loose connections or mistresses. I go into this with an expectation that it persists. Meanwhile, I'm prepared that there may be few and far between women who will accept the model. But who dares nothing, etc. This means that for the two of us to go on a date you need to choose one of the three types.
Christian

Take that. I don't expect to hear back from her ... On to the next.

Dear Christian,
I have been looking for a man of strong will, confidence and power for a long time. If you're man enough to put up such a profile, I am woman enough to want to meet you. Life is too short for small talk and weepers. Meet me Tuesday of next week 4PM at Café Sommersko, and you will get young and fresh company.
Linda

Thank goodness! A woman with grit. How beautiful. Perhaps also because she is not criticizing but is imminent, curious and self-determined. Unless it's all in her keyboard. It will be interesting to meet her, and according to her photo, she is not the dark and exotic, but quite pretty. It suddenly strikes me that this may soon become much more entertaining than I had imagined.

Dear Linda,
You can find me at Sommersko next Tuesday - and if you do not recognize me from the picture, look for a guy who sits alone with a newly opened, cool bottle of Riesling and two glasses.
Christian

The time is approaching half past five and I have not been outside since my run this morning. I think a stroll will do me good ...

On the way to the Freeport and walking home by the Citadel I was in deep thought. Have I thrown myself out in too deep waters? Do I begin to get a little nervous about having to go through a large handful of dates as if I were a teenager again? No, it's something else that bothers me. Although it has been a long time since I split up with my ex-wife, Liva, she continues to haunt my subconscious. Each time I have involved myself with someone, there were memories, and it is impossible not to compare. There were so many good memories, despite the somewhat violent end. We both believed that we had found our respective soul mates. We could talk deeply about everything and did so during long evening hours. Our families and friends did not understand why we broke up, which we didn't when it came down to it – the first time. Because we continued for some time as lovers, although officially we had gone through the legal circus of divorcing. Not that that part was particularly difficult. Basically, there was more paperwork to get married.

Maybe we were too young when we met, but I doubt that excuse now. We were both in our mid-twenties and colleagues a short while. Although our professional lives led us along different tracks, we were a perfect team in all other areas. And since the break I have often been annoyed that I began to feel so bound in the marriage. My suggestion, that we should try to live separately, was obviously perceived as a poorly wrapped call for a complete break, and thus divorce. Despite our ability to communicate intelligently and deeply about all sorts of things, we failed when matters concerned ourselves that way. I was hoping some of that built-up faith in a future together could carry us through, but as the months went by, it became obvious to me that it was an illusion. Better to look back on a divine time and move on, than fight a losing battle for both of us, I finally thought after a lot of wrangling.

A few years ago she rang my doorbell at half past six in the morning because she had lost her keys at a bar and so was a 'damsel in distress'. We found a locksmith, I drove her home via an ATM and paid the two thousand kroner such a service costs. That she had been out drinking and was more than unfortunate is just descriptive of her personality.

But the incident initiated us getting together again as lovers for the second time. However, there was ultimately no alternative but to realize it would not work out – us being life-long partners.

Now she has found a new boyfriend and they even have a daughter. Despite our agreement about not wanting to be parents, she still chose to become a mother and I found that a little strange, but we probably all have a point of view until we redecide. I think she is a good mother.

I still think of her tenderly – a bit like she is a lost sister, or at least a woman I have lost and therefore still miss. There is no doubt my feelings for her includes a good deal of loyalty and probably a portion of love.

When I got home from my thoughtful walk, I read the rest of the responses to my profile. It turned out, however, that the first two I read clearly were the most promising. Apparently there are a number of women in the market, who are either trapped in a super boring marriage, are becoming old virgins or simply have been abandoned in the middle of life. Which is really sad.

Dear Christian,
I think you are just the spice I am missing in my everyday life. My children are grown up and it is a long time ago I was intimate with my husband. I like adventure, so we should meet and have little noncommittal fun. Tell me a little more about your sexual preferences.
Hot possible mistress hugs from Barbara.

Hi Christian,
I'm single again after a marriage that was destined to fail. We never gained the confidence you are looking for – but I totally agree with the fact that there is a soul mate for everyone out there. And I can tell you that I need one. But as I have been disappointed several times by net dating, I think we must begin by writing and then we can perhaps find out which values we can bring into each others' lives.
Loving and expectant greetings,

Anna

I have to decline these invitations, because I am not on a salvation mission here and am forced to stick to my plan to find exactly what I want. Barbara is married and Anna seems too desperate. In other missions, I have usually had success as long as I just kept my focus. And one golden rule is about seeing the positive options. Over the next days there will be more answers, I am sure, because my profile has had much more visitors than there has been replies. The ladies are probably sweating at their keyboards ...

Wednesday 8th September, 2010

Mail From a Real Catch

It's incredible how a full day at the office can pass by not getting stuff done, but at least I finally received input. From unexpected angles, but certainly appreciated.

It started with an email from Marie, whom I curiously enough got to know several years ago, when I also had a dating profile online. At that time, mostly to explore what the concept really meant. There was so much hype in the media that I set out to test it. Apart from a few meaningless dates, I became really good friends with Marie. We quickly discovered that we had a lot in common on the intellectual front and that there was no ground for a sexual relationship. But hours of good, deep conversations should not be underestimated. She moved to Kalundborg a few years ago, away from the city's intensity and we have only had sporadic email contact lately. Typically enough, she wrote now after the summer, from which she attached some wonderful images of her new life. I tease her that she lives in what is the peripheral Denmark. She seems to have had enough of her isolation from the city's pulse, alone with her dog and cat, and she expects to come back, which should be nice enough. Despite my motorcycle, I have not been visiting her enough.

She asks to my everyday life and bitches slightly that I do not keep her updated. But this time I can tell some news:

Dear Marie,
You must have enjoyed the peace out there on the edge. Thank you for the wonderful, visual impressions. In a way, I understand that you miss Copenhagen, and I wonder if the

real estate market may soon give you a reasonable price again? Maybe it's not the best season to sell, but you can probably always find yourself a no-cure-no-pay broker, thus not risking too much financially.

From here I can tell you that I've created a new online dating profile (yes, it is probably a slight surprise to you, I suppose). But this time it's based on a very special model. You see, I'm looking for three different women. It dawned on me that I must listen to a part of my personality that cannot be neglected, because I am attracted to very different sides of women. We have previously discussed the topic, so maybe you're not all that surprised. I was inspired by my friend, Elizabeth, who in the spring set out to find herself three men. You can read about it here: www.onewomanthreemen.com

The key words for me, or the main features if you want, are, respectively, The exotic, My soulmate and the fresh, slightly wild-at-heart type. The project is quite new and I have not yet been on any dates, but it's beginning to take form. Why not be honest and admit that it is extremely rare for two people to fit so well together that they can be everything for each other – at least in our time and culture. It is different when survival depends on people staying together. In more primitive societies where they do not have washing machines, refrigerators or other resources it makes much more sense to share the tasks of a family's daily life. Similarly, some generations ago in our own culture it was the rule rather than the exception that the woman made sure everything worked in the home. Nowadays it is almost embarrassing if one party chooses to be at home for longer periods of time. The resulting stress and lack of mutual dependence ... No, there is no reason to elaborate on this any more. You follow my thoughts, I am sure.

Anyway, this is why I have chosen to engage myself in this with an open mind and I am curious to see how it develops. As you know, I have appreciated to live by myself for a long time now, but the 175 square meter penthouse starts to feel a little empty. And now you will probably ask if I'm going to arrange my penthouse as a harem? Again, I will be honest and say that I do not yet have a golden plan laid out, but am ready to be seduced by the right women. And the first date is next week!
Love Christian

Just as I sent off the mail to Marie, a chat window popped up from Laura, who some years ago was the girlfriend of my good friend, Daniel. They are no longer together, but we can easily find time, all three of us, to meet over a beer at social occasions, and that way we are still in touch. Normally, I see Daniel the most, but I like that Laura has not disappeared completely.

Laura: Hi Christian - are you there?
Christian: Yes, not even working hard ...
Laura: How are you these days? Long time no see!
Christian: Thanks, good, I started a new project - hehe.
Laura: What are you up to?
Christian: I am actively looking for three women - on a dating network!

Just as sudden as she started the chat, her status is now set as away, but I will bet it's because her boss came by and disturbed. It must be so irritating to have a boss. While I wait, I might as well check if there are any new replies.

New catches indeed. And the last to arrive, just minutes ago, matches – magnificently. The profile picture alone makes knees go soft and some other place go hard. Cat's eyes, long, dark curly hair, which appears to go far down her back. An amazing and inviting smile. Her lips are so beautifully formed that I become completely hypnotized there and then. Her glow is like a mixture of honey and nougat. Neither light nor mulatto, but definitely a true latino. Hard to tell if she is from southern Europe or further away, but my heart is almost stopping – or rather, pumping intensely.

In addition she describes herself as an independent woman with a sound economy and a job she sees as her hobby, and these details give her extra points. I definitely have to meet her. Had she included her phone number, I would have called right away.

Hi Karla,
Thank you for your inquiry. You are now first in line and you will be served shortly. In the meantime, I can say that a personal meeting can be arranged and is highly recommended. You have made a big impression already, despite your brief introduction. But I am convinced you will make us both happy if you reserve an hour to meet me for a coffee or a glass of wine in the near future.
Christian

I did not even look through the others, because as expected, Laura resurfaced in the chat window.

Laura: have you gone completely mad?
Christian: LOL - maybe
Laura: Mid-Life Crisis?
Christian: Don't think so – but it's fun and new!

Laura: I must hear more about this soon.
Christian: Will let you know when I'm going out with the guys next time, OK?
Laura: Count me in!

For a long while it's been an informal tradition to meet for beers with three of my friends, Daniel and his cronies, Kasper and Mikkel about once a month. Usually our talks focus on various technical challenges, such as the setup of email servers, selecting the best operating system or showing off the latest gadget - pure male geek stuff. But when Laura once in a while participates, she has a positive effect on conversation topics. We hear little about her two boys for whom Daniel a few years was a great influence as a stepfather. Not that they have been ruined by growing up with only their mother, but Daniel could set limits. Unfortunately, this particular trait – or should I say – this difference between Laura and Daniel, became the main reason why they finally broke up. It is always difficult to enter as a sort of reserve-parent and they are hardly the only one couple in history who, despite good odds, split up in the end. Fortunately, they're still good friends.

Reply from Marie. Not unexpectedly, and nice to get a little encouragement.

Dear, crazy Christian
I know no one like you who can embark on an adventure as exciting and different as this. It irks me even more that I have moved from the capital, for only an idiot would not like to follow the evolution of this project more closely. There is no doubt in my mind, that you will get many replies and you will find out that your profile will be read by many. Women tend to gossip with their friends, when they

consider such a provocative invitation. I would guess that you will find it hard to choose and keep your otherwise always cool overview. Be careful not to get into too troublesome situations. And do promise me a few things. Keep me informed, stay honest to yourself and stay calm in the process. I predict a turbulent time in your life during the next few months.

Your Marie

Oh yes, she is good! I'm sure she's frustrated about not being able to follow the project more closely. But after all, emails are invented for a reason. In the future, at least I have more to talk about than the regular, everyday grind. So I make a mental note that she will get more newsletters from here than previously.

Enough about relationship anguish for today. I need a reunion with The Big Blue. The world's best film and I am privileged to have the long version of the best digital edition. *Between what you know and what you wish, lies the secret of ... The Big Blue!* Jacques, Johana and Enzo, here I come.

Thursday 9th September, 2010

An Exotic and a Fresh

Is it just because autumn has arrived, or have the hours of today simply disappeared? Three meetings at work, one of which might lead to new business on the professional level, but my thoughts have constantly circled on my private project.

I think Marie knows her gender well: The number of visitors to my profile has grown steadily, and I can just imagine how talks are going on in various female friendly gatherings. That is if Marie's theory is correct. It is impossible to verify or prove the case. Unless … Unless I am actually going to go on a date with two women who know each other. That would in fact be pretty entertaining. However, I will keep this assumption to myself. This should preferably not become a social-psychological study.

To my chagrin, there are still many answers clearly coming from unsuitable candidates. Some express themselves as school children, others can not spell or use proper grammar. A few individuals should visit a professional photographer as just the smallest effort to present themselves visually sensible. What was that thought a few days ago, about being picky? Yet more proof that I notice small details and am quite fastidious when it comes down to it. These details become more important in this situation where I can choose hot or not. Had I been on the opposite side of the game, I would surely proofread what I wrote to a woman I wanted to get in contact with.

To my unreserved joy there is a reply from Karla. Apparently she rides on the same day as she saddles. Hmm. Appropriate metaphor?

Dear Christian,
I want to make you happy, and I am quite proud to be first in the line. I will take advantage of this and suggest that we meet for a coffee at Theodor's. Do you know the cozy café? Next Friday afternoon. 4PM would be perfect for me. Would that suit you?
Karla

Brief, bluntly, but with both positive innuendo and the clear certainty that she has several advantages. And Theodor's, it's just around the corner. We can start out with a coffee and continue on more serious matters at my place. And a Friday, I must say the woman kickstarts my fantasies!

Dear Karla,
Theodor's is an excellent choice. The acoustics are good and their selection of coffee more than acceptable. Funny that you should choose that place because I live in the immediate vicinity and visit the place often. The timing is well chosen too, and it should be easy to find space in an adequate cozy corner. If it becomes crowded later on, we can always continue at my place.
See you next Friday,
Christian

I wonder whether it is too intrusive to mention the possibility of going home to my place following coffee? Well. She does seem, after all, as a girl who appreciates action, so it can hardly hurt to give the option. Off goes my answer.

Starting to think whether she might even have been at Theodor's, and seen me there? And I just have not noticed her? No, I would always notice a woman with her face, although I could have been sitting with my back to the entrance, and she might have seen me in a mirror? Well, does not matter. In one week and one day I will become wiser on Karla.

On to the next ...

Hi Christian,

Maybe your first thought when you see me is that I am too young for you. However, I hope you will read all my words before you decide whether to respond or throw me in the trash, electronically speaking.

I have just started studying media sciences after some years in South America, where I traveled around and worked for a living. Already as a young girl, that is: even younger, I knew that it was necessary for me to experience foreign cultures. It never suited me follow the so-called normal routine of going through high school and directly continue on to the university. However, it has always been a part of my plan to study. So therefore, yes: I am a student now. I hope you understand this does not imply a very young and naive creature, because I have a solid foundation thanks to my years away from the little pond we call Denmark.

My dilemma is that it can be unreasonably difficult to find worthy adversaries among my fellow students, and a natural consequence of my stay abroad is that I only have a sparse social circle. Until now that is, because when I read your profile, I felt an immediate curiosity to get to know you better. But I also understand if you just laugh while reading this. I could almost be your daughter.

It is not a fatherfigure, I'm looking for, but a mature man who has found a balance in his life. That you are looking for three different types of women does not frighten me, and I shall not present to say that I match any of your wishes. As you can see, I am certainly not your exotic type. And I don't see myself as a comfort addict, although some security always is nice, perhaps even necessary. So if I have to choose, I bid in as number three, but have a feeling that you invented the last type in order to hit three in total. But I could be wrong, and there is probably only one way to find out: By initiating a dialogue with you. This first step is a start.

Hope to hear from you

Best regards, Sabine

My first thought when I see the excellent picture of Sabine is that she certainly is young. Her eyes and inscrutable little smile beams of a warm and deep self-assurance, but also a freshness you only see in people who still have a good proportion of youth to go before the conflictual adulthood sets in in earnest. The picture could have been the inspiration for Leonardo, before he painted the Mona Lisa, even though the girl in no way looks like his model. Sabine's qualities lie more in a somewhat mystical purity and open curiosity. Her picture is missing only the hint of a light-ring, and I would have sworn that she is the closest resemblance I have ever seen of an angel.

Her words also left me deeply impressed. She must be around thirty, at most, and still she possesses a mature self-awareness, appropriate amounts of irony and humor and not least a wonderful ability to write fluently and accurately.

Hi Sabine,

Your letter made a deep impression on me, thanks for sending it. Not just your words but also your portrait leaves me with very warm feelings and I am more than excited to get to know you better. You are extremely articulate and in addition a visual delight, so I hope we can continue at a café and not just through written exchanges.

I myself, many years ago, lived in Brazil for 18 months and am curious to hear more about where in South America you have been. I also like your little ironic mini-analysis of my definition of female types. And frankly, you may have a point. But my point is that I know myself well enough now to realize some important facts. For example, it doesn't work if I have to change parts of my personality to adapt to a partner. Then I become someone I'm not. Similarly, I don't ask of a partner or girlfriend, that she should obey me. One should stick to own beliefs and feel whole in oneself. That, hopefully, does not lead to always being oneself and only one, right?

In subtle ways I already have a feeling that you understand what I mean and I look forward to continuing our dialogue.

Now at least you know that I have not thrown you in the trash. Rather, you just skipped to the top of the board, and I would like to be your worthy adversary, engage in dialogue and anything else I can dig up you may need.

Christian

Friday 10th September, 2010

New, But Old Father

It has been awhile since I last spent an evening with good, old Nikolai. Fortunately, we can both be spontaneous, and this morning we agreed to meet for beers 4:30PM at the Berlin Bar. He lives nearby with his wife, Rosa, who became his girlfriend nearly three years ago when they met via, yes you guessed it: Online dating! They are the only couple that I know who seems to have prolonged success with the concept. In the sense that not only did they marry but now also have a daughter, Erica, just over a year old.

Nikolai and I know each other from high school and happened to meet again many years later. The years without contact would eventually prove to be insignificant, because it seemed like just the other day, although much had happened in the meantime. After some time being single he had reached a point where he started doing online dating. And now he's become a father in the rather mature age of almost fifty. This can create many funny stories, and usually he starts our conversation following an identical pattern of complaints, disease and sleep deprivation.

- Phew, what a week this has been. I am completely trashed! He said, and thus fulfilled my expectations.

- Haha. Erica has been sick again?

- Not just her, we have all three been hit by a new virus. I have hardly slept for almost two weeks.

- I've heard about this from others. Is it something to do with daycare?

- We have kept her at home since we pulled her away from the last one. Didn't I tell you about that?

I had probably heard the story, but he continued.

- They left the gate wide open. There was no control of anything, and we chose to sign up at a new place. Maybe they avenged themselves by simply giving Erica an extra virus to take home on the last day.

Nikolai is still in a combination of parental leave and job search. But basically he is glad to have started a family. I cannot help but tease him a little about his decisions, and there is no doubt that it is a lot smarter to have children much earlier in life. Firstly, we can cope with the interrupted sleep periods better, and secondly, I also believe you are less fussy about a baby as a younger parent. The fact you're going to be among the oldest parents when the child grows up, is probably a minor detail, because in a flock of siblings the youngest kid will always have middle-aged parents. But if you have been free and childless most of your adult life the change and the pressure is much more serious. Nikolai and his Rosa are the ultimate proof. My own decision to stay childless is confirmed every time I hear about their challenges.

- Don't you miss teaching, getting out amongst others and such? You surely cannot spend every day walking in the Frederiksberg Gardens and pottering about Erica?

- Until we get Erica in a new daycare, I have no choice. It erodes my financial capital and we have dropped finding a bigger apartment.

- As I read the other day: "Three minutes of happiness and eighteen years of obligation."

- Or how about: "Sometimes it's quick, at other times it takes three minutes."

Fortunately his mood improves when he exploits the opportunity to get out a little and vent the sophomoric humor. Unlike some of my other friends our talks often focus on women. Nikolai is one of the most sex-fixated people I know. In a good way, but I can still marvel. Sometimes I think he goes around in a perpetual malnutrition, and it must be slightly difficult to maintain the frequency of the past, now they have a baby at home. A standard comment is "Can you imagine the woman over there without any clothes? I bet she shaves it." Or the classic moment when his attention in the middle of a sentence makes a small leap to follow a cute behind, walking past us.

- By the way, I have recently created a dating profile ...

- Aha, as I always say: "Out of the woman came the man, and he has kept trying to get back ever since."

- Yes and no. It is a bit of an experiment. I've written that I'm looking for three different women. Or types in the least.

- A harem! Finally you take revenge! Have you received any replies?

- Oh yes. Although there are many dimwits, but next week I am meeting a few dates, and there is ongoing dialogues with some others.

- What types are you looking for?

- In short, I want The Exotic, My Soulmate and The Fresh, a little wild-at-heart. I started to realize that these qualities could never exist in a single woman and I'm attracted to them all. So why not give it a try?

- You know that you risk a lot of hassle, right?

- Yes, but I'll also get a lot of fun. Anyway, I've had enough beer, let's go out and find some more solid foods.

I did not exactly need to be reminded of all the potential problems I might run into during the project. Our dinner conversation continued about the life of a new, but old father. Preparing food, bathing, playing and God knows what. Maybe I should have used the same phrase about a lot of hassle when he first told me that he was to be a father.

Monday 13th September, 2010

Three Dates Planned

The day has passed by preparing my motorcycle for the winter. You never know when the final trip of the year has suddenly come and gone, and I hate washing, waxing and polishing with my fingers freezing off. The bike is good for another ride or two this season, but if doesn't happen until spring, all is set for hibernation in the garage. In a way, it is rather silly that I have not sold it, with my extremely minimal consumption of gasoline and thus mileage covered. But ever since I can remember, I've always seen myself as the owner of a motorcycle as an adult. Much more deliberate and focused than to imagine or wish for kids. It is in no way a substitute, and a combination could probably also be done. Just without a sidecar. And as life has evolved, it was fortunately the more targeted dream, I realized.

There is also some mental cleansing involved in maintaining such a machine. Not that I inevitably experience a Zen-like mode, but still. Thoughts float freely and beautifully when I'm puttering about it with the suitable shampoo and Turtle Wax.

The image of Karla was stuck on my retina. I imagine that she has an affectionate voice and a fixed gaze. She is probably also the type who does not hold herself back from playing with her hair during a conversation. More or less consciously, but we all know which signals that sends. Do I believe that we end up at my place? It would be appropriate because we meet on a Friday. The timing will be appropriate for me to invite her home for an impromptu – or so it can be presented – homemade meal. I must remember to ensure I have stocked up some adequate supplies.

I am also curious about my appointment with Linda tomorrow at Sommersko, but there is not quite the same potential. Based on her photo, she is definitely not the exotic type, but nice and sober-looking. She basically looks a little like Ally McBeal, representing a completely different style than the exotic. This leads me to think maybe I should perform a little research.

After having some pasta and pouring an extra glass of red wine, I sat down to investigate how much I could find out about Linda. Some time ago I met a Frenchman who has helped develop some pattern recognition software, and I agreed to help out testing for them. With the portrait of Linda as a seed, I got the program to look for similar motifs on the net. I had barely put the glass to my mouth before a virtual sea of images turned up on my screen. Effective software!

At first glance it was like seeing a gallery of Calista Flockhart, alone in different postures, at gala dinners and with or without Mr. Ford. But interesting and impressive enough, the very first image was identical with the dating profile photo of Linda. Not just another portrait, but the very same. When I clicked on it, I was referred to the website of a law firm in Copenhagen. Imagine that. She has used her image from a professional contact page as her online dating photo - equal parts honesty as somewhat naive.

But for me a very important side benefit. She is a partner in the company, which I interpret as two immediate bonus points: Firstly, she must have a reasonably healthy economy and is not a gold-digger. There are so many women who are looking for economic security in a man. Have they learned nothing from the past several years while fighting for equality? I am happy to be polite and pay the bill when we go to a restaurant and so on. But it does not quite do when they base their future on being a kept woman. That ends the mutual respect and brings us back to the past, which cannot be right.

The second point, I could assign to Linda, was the fact that she as a lawyer and also a partner, may conceivably be both independent-minded and relatively busy with her job. That means she is not one to lazy about in the sofa, not one to play housewife and not one who is lacking input in everyday life. She may even, depending on her secrecy clause, supply some exciting stories from his own life. And it never hurts to have a close contact with people such as accountants, lawyers and other advisers. Hey, I might get my very own private lawyer?

She will also be well-dressed, educated, exceptionally articulate. Or is my imagination just going wild by seeing her portrait?

There is some truth to us men being visually orientated. Both images of Karla and Linda have almost led me to define how each of them are as women. Qualities that I in no way know anything about and our respective written exchanges have also been quite brief. Normally I would prefer to write a little more and let a woman express herself on several topics, but it has only been the young Sabine, who appeared to be effective at the keyboard. And the mysterious Lizzy was almost anti-informative. Moreover, it is nearly a week ago I wrote her back, so my prediction that she would pull out seems verified. Or maybe she cannot decide which type she has to bid for.

I sincerely hope that Nikolai's statements from last Friday don't contain a kind of curse. It may already be quite a task to keep the women separate, but my calendar has room for more. Should I choose, I would probably rather hear from Sabine again in order to meet her face to face.

It dawns on me that I have not checked my profile and if I had believed more in supernatural abilities, it was a really good day, because Sabine has been at her keyboard.

Dear Christian,
I am curious what you can dig up for me. Thank you for your long answer and that you did not write off me in advance. I was also around in Brazil, but the last several months of my stay in South America was in Argentina, the land of good steaks and superb red wine. That is far more appealing than milk and honey to me.
How about meeting up an evening next week? It seems that we can certainly find many things to talk about.
Love Sabine

There is a god! She could not have phrased it better in my eyes. Not too long, extremely relevant references to our earlier dialogue and ready to meet. And she is not afraid to eat red meat. That's my girl.

Dear Sabine,
My mouth is watering already. Let's meet at the MASH restaurant on Thursday at 7PM. I have already booked a table for us. But let us start out with a cocktail in the bar first, this way your arrival doesn't need to be super accurate, I'll be there before you. It is impolite having a woman wait.
Sincerely,

Christian

Oh, I must remember to let the bad pickup lines stay at home, but it is hard to avoid those about heaven must be missing an angel. I can hardly wait to see the inscrutable smile in real life. And speaking of manners, pick-up lines etc, I will not hold myself back from giving her compliments. She is sufficiently young to still be blushing instead of thinking: "Old fool." I hope. After all, it was her initiating the contact well knowing that I am older, but not yet an old fool.

Amazingly, there was a response from Lizzy too. Not surprisingly, one of the ultra-short form.

Dear Christian,
I agree that times have changed our assumptions and our ways to engage in relationships. Possibly even agree with your observation that it may be an idea to fill your needs by more than "the one and only". I would like to bid in as a soul mate candidate and suggest we grab a cup of coffee at the French Café Tuesday afternoon. Would 3PM be good for you?
Love Lizzy

Okay, now things are heating up. Four arrangements in the book and it's just a week ago I put my profile on the net! In a way, I am happy to be fastidious, and that I have been able to weed out with a clear conscience. Well, it may seem rude to not respond to inquiries, but that's the rule of the game in online dating. If I have offended some women, I can only hope for them that they have better luck with others, or that they aim widely and do not take my silence as an overly serious defeat.

In return, I am reasonably satisfied with the outcome and look forward to meeting at least two of the four catches. Not that Linda and Lizzy necessarily are less interesting, but Karla and Sabine are higher on my list.

The sequence is also quite perfect: Linda tomorrow, then Sabine on Thursday, Karla on Friday and Lizzy on Tuesday of next week. I almost hope there will be a period of silence in my profile inbox.

Tuesday 14th September, 2010

The First Date

Sommersko keeps their good style. The first authentic café in the country, and despite periods of excessively arrogant staff and too many guests, I was pleasantly surprised and almost nostalgic, already when I entered the door a little to four this afternoon.

A spontaneous impulse prompted me to order Chablis instead of their Riesling and I found a table along the wall so I could watch the entrance. She would hardly notice that I had chosen another wine. I deliberately decided against reading a newspaper, so as not to give myself a certain political direction, and instead I sat down to check emails on my phone. As it dawned on me that I could appear as a nerd who sits and plays brain dead games, I put it in my pocket just as I saw what could easily be Calista Flockhart's younger sister on a straight path to my table. Targeted as a heat-seeking, or in this context a white wine-seeking missile.

I got up to pull out her chair.

- Welcome and thanks for suggesting Sommersko. It's just as nice as in the old days, I said.

- Yes, it is actually quite a while since I was here, but they keep their style.

Was there a kind of ESP between us? I had just had the same thought ... I poured her a glass of the chilled wine.

- Didn't you mention you'd be having a Riesling? How did you know that I clearly prefer Chablis?

- I have my skills, I said and winked at her.

- Well, then ... cheers, then.

She lifted her glass, and I saw that her hand trembled slightly as she took a cautious sip. But even the strongest personalities are probably somewhat excused on a first date. I shrugged it off.

After we had exchanged a few generalities about the weather, parking in the middle of downtown and other small talk, we slowly entered into more personal details. She relaxed a bit more, and I watched her with pleasure. Her smooth hair was well groomed. As expected, she dressed tastefully feminine, which in my dictionary means an elegant suit over a silk blouse. No jewelry except some very discreet ear studs in gold. Her long fingers seemed to have just come from a manicure treatment, or at least undergo regular and expensive care. She was the epitome of high-maintenance. Perfectly fine with me.

- So you are a partner in a law firm, I understand?

- What? How do you know? Tell me, have you made a sort of research on me?

- Well, it is ... It was not that hard to figure out. Your photo on the profile is the same as on your corporate website, I said and chose to keep the sneaky, French software outside the topic. She was already paranoid enough.

- What else do you know about me? And the wine preference...?

- No, listen. The whole thing is a bit of a collection of coincidences and you cannot blame me for being curious during the week. I thought it was great to be meeting a girl of your character. You seem focused and proactive.

- You can bet on that. I did not hide the fact that I go after a man who can provide me a worthy opponent. But you're avoiding my questions. What do you know about me and how did you find out?

- Well, I do not know more than you are a partner in the law firm, honestly!

- So you're after money, eh? Let me inform you that I am about to knock off a debt of half a million.

- Haha. You don't have to make up weird stories, honey. Money is not everything.

- You do not call me "honey". I will say thanks for the wine – but not necessarily au revoir.

Aha. It was a very sweet ass now walking toward the door, leaving me to sit there with almost a whole bottle of good wine and a whole lot to think about. I was completely indifferent to people around me staring. It was not an angry girlfriend who left, or a too loud quarrel, which led to her sudden exit.

What have I done wrong here?

First and foremost, I decided not to engage in investigating my upcoming dates – neither using French software nor

Google. It is clearly better to be surprised. Well, I got surprised today, but still.

Perhaps it is also an idea to hold back using cute nicknames until there's slightly more rapport between my date and me. It seemed like the last straw when I called her honey, and obviously I should have been more careful. She apparently had much more need for someone who could put her in place than someone who was at most her equal. That is not how I see myself, one to put a woman in place. Women should preferably discover that a relationship needs to be balanced, and no party needs to have the most power. But we are all different, I suppose.

Conclusion of the first date:
1. Do not research in advance, let yourself be surprised
2. Beware of using loving words too soon
3. I really wasn't much wiser ...

But what could I expect when our conversation only lasted for about twenty minutes, and she was very nervous from the start? Already the day after tomorrow, I have Sabine on the menu, which hopefully will be a better experience.

Gosh, what if that ends just as badly just as quickly ... Then I can sit abandoned with red wine and two large steaks. No, easy now! Our correspondence so far has been promising, and a girl with such an innocent face cannot possibly be complicated during a few hours. Furthermore, I look forward to Friday when the fantastically beautiful Karla shows up at Theodor's.

It was a good thing I had walked to Sommersko, because when I had finally finished philosophizing over almost a whole Chablis, it did me well to catch a little fresh air on the way home.

Basically, I think I will skip dinner and instead look forward to enjoying a decent brunch with Benjamin tomorrow morning. We will meet at the Hilton Hotel and plan to spend some good hours at their outstanding buffet.

Wednesday 15th September, 2010

A Different Kind of Marriage

I first met Benjamin fifteen years ago. About ten years ago, he married a girl from the Philippines. Not the typical mail-order bride, she was already living in Denmark. For one reason or another, or maybe even more, I have always found their marriage a bit too exotic for my model. For instance, they mostly communicate in English because her Danish is still somewhat limited. If they both spoke English as an equal standard language like his Danish and her Tagalog, it would not be a problem. But they lose so many nuances, when their English is a language learned at school long ago. Even with the big media influence from Hollywood on both Denmark and the Philippines, communication is never the same as with a fully shared language.

But Benjamin's wife is an excellent cook. She takes very good care of him. She remains in the background, almost to the point of embarrassment under Danish conditions. He is well aware that it cannot be compared to a traditional Danish marriage. But if she'd rather watch TV, read or be social with her friends, it's fine with him, and they are a happy couple.

One consequence of this is that Benjamin has built up a stockpile of items he is eager to talk about when we meet. There is much to discuss, including Bjorn Lomborg's views, the immigration policy, new scientific discoveries and sometimes even more esoteric topics such as fate and the meaning of life. Today was no different.

- Well, it's too damn bad that Germany, one of our close neighbors, sits on radioactive waste without controlling the decay process better, he said.

- You may be right, but at least BarsebŲck closed down, didn't it? And that is much closer to us.

- The waste is a much, much bigger problem. They are beginning to do better and safer operations, but imagine the 24 kilograms of plutonium, which is located in a salt mine below Asse. With a half life of 24 thousand years, the material will remain lethal for more than a million years. And they expect that mine will last no more than 10 years. That's when the groundwater starts to become contaminated.

Benjamin sometimes has difficulty remembering phone numbers, street names and other generalities, but when it comes to matters that concern him, the more autistic sides of his memory fire up.

- Ten years? That's the day after tomorrow, seen in the large context. But as far as I know, nobody has found the perfect storage for nuclear waste.

- No, and that is why we should investigate more into renewable energy. If you placed the barrels from the warehouse under Asse on a field, they would fill up more than fifteen football fields.

Rainman strikes again.

- But the problem with renewable energy is that power must be transported a long way before it reaches consumers, right?

On and on went the discussion, or rather conversation, because we did not disagree. Just more proof that he does not have an outlet for these kind of considerations at home with his wife. I appreciate such intellectual dialogues, and it is one of the things I still miss from my time with Liva. It took no more than a story in the news, or an article in the newspaper and we would spend hours weighing the pros and cons. Challenge each other's views. Laugh and be indignant about this and that. Together.

During the time after our final break my friends have given me ample opportunities to receive input and food for thought, but it is different with a life-long partner with whom you can build an ever larger and more robust, common understanding. Grow together and enjoy mutual respect grow.

It also requires adjustment; there will always be areas where you have to find a compromise. And that's what makes relationships so complicated. Even with the best intentions of making things work, the balance between compromise and adaption and maintaining one's own identity, is subtle and often unattainable.

That adultery in many cases is the final nail in the coffin, was fortunately not the case with my marriage. Had that happened, we would probably not have continued to be lovers after the divorce. Despite the fact that we both should have known better, it was physically impossible to turn off the switch. We probably both continued to covet each other

in the sexual area. Good memories, all the way till the end –
I have to admit that.

Another thing I might as well admit is that I could not
expect particularly deep response from my male friends
about my project of finding three women. When I tried to
bring it up with Benjamin, his response was almost
predictable.

- That sounds fun. Are there any good babes out there?

- To be quite honest, I am worried that so many are totally
uninteresting, to me, anyway. But I'm seeing a few
tomorrow and the day after, so my hopes are up.

- Cool for you. Have fun.

And that was it. There is probably some truth to all the
articles in various magazines. Men tend to talk less about
emotions and stuff like that. It makes me even gladder that
my world also contains good, close female friendships. And
I must remember to keep Marie oriented. She's going to kill
me if she moves back to Copenhagen, and there has been
development she doesn't know about in the project. It is also
about time to gather the guys for beer again, and I will check
with Laura if she's still on.

At any rate: The next two days will provide more content:
Sabine and Karla.

Thursday 16th September, 2010

The Second Date

MASH was filled to the brim. I do not understand there is still talk of an economic crisis. This place is not cheap, and in addition to a full house and waiting customers at the bar, I noticed that everyone was dressed as for a gala. I was incredibly excited to meet Sabine while I sat and sipped my Dry Martini near the entrance.

There was a rather high level of noise, but I had secured myself a table inside at a corner, so we could talk undisturbed. While I watched the other visitors and in particular studied the appetizers, which were served here in the bar, I could feel my stomach began to rumble. Lovely to feel hunger and butterflies.

Suddenly Sabine stood beside me, held out her hand and smiled.

- Good evening, Christian.

She was slightly taller than I had expected. Her hair was more vigorous than in the picture I had seen. Her eyes and smile more alive. But that was no wonder, here she was in real life and looked so vibrantly beautiful.

- Hello Sabine. I have taken the liberty of ordering a Dry Martini for you, have a seat here before we go to our table. It should be ready in a moment.

- Wonderful, I have a really healthy appetite. Cheers.

We both had, that much became apparent soon. We agreed to order a selection of accessories to share, so we could try out many culinary offerings. As I had hoped and expected, there was more quiet in here at the back of the restaurant, and the atmosphere was pleasant and relaxed. Aided by satisfied diners and subdued, well-chosen ambient music from discreetly placed speakers.

- It's actually a little comical. I chose MASH inspired by Argentina, and now we end up eating Danish meat and drinking red wine from Chile, I explained.

- Quite all right to me. It is a lovely wine, and I appreciate the local produce wherever in the world I find myself.

- How long ago is it you were in Argentina?

- I've been home for some months and have just started at the University here at the beginning of September.

- So the next three years will be spent with a bachelor's or what?

- Do you see yourself as the bachelor?

- Hehe. Technically, I do not fall into that category, since I have been married.

The evening and the conversation was better than I could hope for. Sabine proved to be an only child and had lost her parents. Thanks to a respectable inheritance, she had a healthy economy, but not much family. There was an uncle living on Nekseloe where she kept most of her furniture. She lived in a rented room in Classensgade and for good reason spent most of her time studying.

- I may be alone, but I'm never lonely, she said, and flashed the sweetest smile to me.

- That's how I see my own life. But in the long run I may still be missing some intimacy. That was why I decided on my online dating profile.

- And the same reason I chose to write to you, I believe.

She seemed very reflective. The warm feeling of a desire to protect began to emerge in me. Here was a girl I could be seriously happy with. You can't put a finger on her perfect exterior. Or rather: I would love to let my fingers explore every square inch of her shapely body. When she held her head slightly tilted to consider her next sentence, I had to pull myself together not to caress her neck. Luckily the table was just wide enough that I could not reach across. I reminded myself to proceed slowly.

- What a wonderful dinner. I have no room for dessert, but how about we quietly walk back home? I actually live just a few blocks further out and would like to follow you home safely.

- Hahaha. After my stay in South America, I am not nervous about walking alone through Copenhagen. But it's an excellent suggestion. I took the bus here, because I haven't yet bought a bike.

Even her laugh was so beautiful and melodious that I bubbled inside. On the trip home I considered inviting her up for a nightcap, but held on to my decision to be a bit cautious. It was sufficient to ask for her mobile number as we stood at the door of her building.

My second date has been a clear success. Especially in comparison with the first, and my only grievance now is that we have not made a new appointment. However, I should not forget that Karla is on the program tomorrow afternoon. Sabine was correct in pointing out that she herself was not exactly the exotic type, and there is no doubt that Karla fully meets that requirement - at least photographically. There is a little Salma Hayek in her, or Penelope Cruz, which is absolutely not to be despised.

I must say that Elizabeth has sparked something here. Had it not been for her new model, I hardly would have come to this. Oddly enough, I can also recognize some of her anguish, because during dinner with Sabine, already on the first date with her, I began thinking of the one and only. Could she outweigh my desire for all of them? Not that I believe in a creator, but could she be the one created to contain everything for me?

Friday 17th September, 2010

The Third Date

In the absence of an espresso machine at home, I often enjoy to order this exquisite beverage, and preferably the double shot, when I'm at Theodor's. I had only tasted one sip when I saw Karla make her entrance. And heard her high heels clicking as she approached my table. All of the other café guests eyed her closely and I got up with a big, friendly smile.

- Welcome to my second living room, I said and gave her a hug which she returned closely and long enough to be nice without becoming awkward.

- Thank you. You have arranged yourself comfortably here. Will you offer me a cup of chocolate?

- Naturally. With or without whipped cream?

- With, please. But no extra sugar.

When I went up to the bar to place the order, I saw in a mirror that Karla took off her jacket and sat down with her long, shapely legs crossed. She was wearing a tight black dress with a deep cut not leaving much to the imagination. It would possibly be hard to maintain her gaze for longer periods. She, in turn, would be guaranteed to keep many eyes staring, as long as she was there.

- Here you go, whipped cream and without extra sugar. That would probably be too sweet.

- Yes, I'm sweet enough as is. Her smile and voice alike were ultra seductive.

- Extravagant dress, it suits you really well.

- Thank you. It is my own design, I have a clothing store up in Hellerup.

- Wow. Impressive. I mean, that is a tough industry?

- In the beginning, yes. But since my first customers began to recommend me to girlfriends, everything picked up. I have two part time employees, so I can now concentrate on my hobbies, namely to design and enjoy life's pleasures.

There was perhaps an ill-disguised allusion in the latter part of the sentence? When she was distracted by a passing ambulance outside, I devoured the sight of her cleavage. The black lace of her bra was visible, I could feel the urge to get in close contact grew rapidly. Mentally I was already starting to strip her in my own room to soft jazz. Or maybe a little hot samba.

We talked a little more about generalities such as the challenges of being self-employed, but most of the time I could tell that we both had our thoughts elsewhere.

Her long, dark curly hair nicely caressed her shoulders, and so far the only negative part was that she had artificial nails. Alternatively, she had an abnormally high level of calcium. I believe I'm able to spot these kinds of devices, and usually it is a bit of a minus, but here I would have to bend the rules. That her perfume was somewhat overwhelming, too, could probably be solved by starting the further process in my

Jacuzzi. A glass of wine in the living room while the water is filling up .. She would be in for a real treat, and I looked forward to a lathering up such a perfect body. Preferably more than once, and preferably with a subsequent rub in body lotion.

My thoughts and our conversation was interrupted as her phone rang.

- Do answer it, being self-employed, it may be a customer.

She looked knowingly at me while she took off her left earring and answered the call.

- Hiii Charlie-love ... Nooo, you know me better than that. My times at cafés are over. I'm just out with the girls to get a little inspiration ... We might stay out for dinner, so you can just manage for yourself and Sebastian tonight ... Yes, yes. That is fine. See you later.

Charlie-love and Sebastian?

- That was my husband. He just picked up Sebastian from the kindergarten and wanted to know whether I was in the shop or at home.

- So you are married and have a son?

- Yes, nothing unusual about that, is there?

- No, OK. Marriage as an institution is not quite dead, but am I terribly mistaken or have we been flirting quite mutually here?

- You're in no way mistaken. And I enjoy every moment. I have noticed how your eyes have caressed me already.

- Does your husband know that you're lying to him?

- I do not think we should get into that. Your espresso is over, and my chocolate has gotten cold. How about a glass of wine?

- No, I'm sorry. As attractive you are, this is just too wrong to go forward. We've probably had the same thoughts along the way, but with completely different backgrounds.

- Are you backing out just because I am married?

- Call me old fashioned, but I will not be the cause of another man's misfortune. If you do not have enough in him, I think it is wrong for you to be married.

To my own surprise, I was absolutely in no doubt here. She was a sight for gods and adult men. It could be quite enjoyable to realize scenes that just minutes earlier had been playing out in my mind. But it dawned on me that Karla is a woman who is lying and most likely a cold-blooded seducer, even though she looks like a very hot lady. I prefer to be able to trust a woman.

- How unfortunate. But thanks for the brief meeting, and here is my card if you change your mind in the future.

I didn't follow her out, but remained sitting a little to think about the last hour of events. Not many seconds had elapsed from the time she came in the door until I had the first hot thoughts about her in an intimate situation. During our relatively short conversation we had sent strong signals, I was in no doubt about that, and she had even confirmed the mutual attraction when she walked out. I could not help thinking whether I had missed out on an invaluable experience by sticking to my principles. It all fell at Checkpoint Charlie.

On the way home I decided to write an update to Marie. That would purify my mind and address the unresolved, which was also a result of this date number three. What a disappointment that Karla was a woman you cannot trust. I do not need to be the only one but I demand honesty from a woman.

Dear Marie,
Now I've been on three dates. Very entertaining and highly varied experiences, not least because I also learn a lot about myself. The latest this afternoon was an eye opener in a double sense. She was pretty as a southern princess, but it dawned on me that she was a bit of a liar and possibly serially unfaithful to her husband. I would guess she is one of those who has multiple affairs going outside her marriage. There is bound to be a lot of men who will gladly obey her wishes, but I'm not one of them.

It is reassuring to find out I have my limits. Yesterday's date was in stark contrast. Her name is Sabine and she is somewhat young, I admit that right away. But she is clever and has traveled a lot. She is studying media sciences and she seems ambitious. In her own words she might fall a little outside the categories, but there is a good chemistry, I cannot ignore. We communicate well together and her body is nice and crispy. No, I did not get into close contact yet, so save me your comments.

The first date was last Tuesday (yes, busy week) and was a complete failure. After a short time I accidentally offended her. It was a combination of unfortunate circumstances and the fact that she perhaps was a little paranoid. The only thing that irks me is that she would be good to know better, her being a lawyer. Overall I am pretty satisfied, and when I am finished writing you in a minute, I will send a text message to Sabine. Her, I need to see more, and the sooner the better!

Have a nice weekend
Christian.

Monday 20th September, 2010

Hooked Already?

Over the weekend I exchanged a good handful of text messages with Sabine, and we finally agreed to meet again this evening and go for a walk around the Citadel. She spends most of her time with books and watching movies as part of her studies, so I cannot help but be a bit envious: Films and books and then hand over some papers once in a while. What a luxury study. For my part, I have spent most of my career in the school of life. A good result is measured on recurring clients and their recommendations to new contacts. It could be fun to have a PhD on my business card, but usually when I have encountered people with long university educations, I have seen them as too theoretical. Often they lack insight into reality and experience of the always changing business life. With Sabine it's different and that is not only due to the fact that she has been out and about in the world. She has only just begun her long study and cannot be compared to bookworms who have lived between five and ten years in the protected atmosphere of a university.

However, she can be compared to my ex, Liva. Among the common features is their ability to lead a comfortable conversation. I find an even greater inner peace with Sabine despite her young age. I have rarely met a girl under the age of thirty, exuding such a degree of the wonderful combination of peace and self-esteem. Even when I was married to Liva, and should have given her confidence in our common life, she could sometimes be insecure. It took no more than a glance from a passing woman, which I usually never even was aware of, before Liva accused me of being a womanizer. At the beginning with a twist of humor, but as the years went by, it became an increasing challenge, or even a bother. If I am not even noticing those eyes that were threatening Liva, I could only become stressed. I had a feeling this would be different with Sabine.

On the evening trip with her around the Citadel I truly enjoyed her company and not least the sight of a picturesque glow of autumn in the beautiful sunset with some impressive clouds. Such a vision always makes me think about how cool it is to fly. A good evening for a pilot to approach a landing in Kastrup, I would think.

- Have you ever dreamed you could fly? She asked, looking at the pretty cumulus clouds, and I caught myself thinking she almost read my thoughts.

- Yes, it is a recurring dream. Fortunately, because that is a fantastic feeling, but I also love the ones, where I can swim underwater without the need to breathe.

I grabbed the chance and wanted to investigate whether she was ready to talk about topics that show insight into how the subconscious represents images of a person's personality.

- I know those, too. Being able to move around in all three dimensions and navigate freely. I wonder if it is a sign of confidence and being ambitious?

- Yes, I've read a few books on the interpretation of dreams, and occasionally I can get quite disappointed that many of my dreams are easy to understand.

- But self-insight is surely both healthy and rewarding?

- Definitely. I would just like to be more intrigued sometimes.

- You can try a technique I learned from a good friend in Argentina. It is about being very aware that you fall asleep. That way you can achieve to double-dream.

- Double-dream?

- Yes, it sounds strange but it works. When you dream that way, you may find that you fall asleep again, or into a deeper level. You could call it "ultra lucid dreaming" and the effect is that you're aware that you are dreaming.

- Aha, I know that feeling well. It can be pretty spooky sometimes, because you can become quite confused.

- It just takes a little practice. My friend down there, her name is Judy, but she's called the dream-girl, was pretty good at introducing me to the technique.

We continued a little along the same tracks, without exchanging concrete dreams stories. I thought it was too early to go into such personal details. Apparently, she felt the same way, but there was undoubtedly the basis for many rewarding conversations to come. And she received more points in my virtual grade book.

At one point we sat on a bench and enjoyed the twilight, and a few minutes without conversation was not even awkward. She broke the silence with a question that caught me by surprise.

- How are things going with your project to find three women?

Of course she had not forgotten the moronic profile text. I had spent the weekend mostly thinking of her and slowly warming up to a reunion. There had admittedly been a few more inquiries, but no one interesting enough to follow up on. Or maybe it's because I've had Sabine on my mind almost the entire time.

- Well ... I've met a few besides you, but none of them can match the feeling you give me. It is as if I've already known you long while, and at the same time I have a huge desire to get to know you much better. And I would even like that to take some time.

- I completely follow you there. You are nice to talk to, and you help me relax.

She moved up close, either because the season caused cooler evenings or because she was not afraid to show initiative. Maybe a mix, but it was signal enough for me to put my arm around her shoulder. For a moment the setting sun broke through the clouds and lit them from below. It was so beautiful a sight, that I got quite tearful eyes and pulled Sabine closer to me. Her hair, which was neither light nor dark, but had this unique glow of naturally light stripes, smelled heavenly. She must have noticed that I breathed deeply, inhaling her bouquet, and she slowly turned her face toward mine. Never before has a first kiss been so good.

We sat closely for a long while and walked slowly all the way back to Classensgade. Along the way, I seriously wondered whether I should invite her home with me instead of dropping her off to her rented room. On the other hand it was a Monday evening and she is busy with her reading. I have an important meeting early tomorrow, so it was with a warm and long kiss, we said our goodbyes. And with an agreement to meet again soon. She was curious to see how I live, so it was natural to invite her to dinner, but unfortunately it can't be until Friday.

On the short way home a familiar warmth spread throughout my body. I smiled at the thought of having Sabine over for dinner and could not wait until Friday. It suddenly struck me that I am to meet with the mysterious Lizzy tomorrow afternoon, and almost wanted to cancel. Nevertheless, it would be something of a cop-out for my master plan, and who knows ... There are many fish in the lake.

Tuesday 21st September, 2010

The Fourth Date

In the lakes of Copenhagen there aren't many fish, but down at the French Café is one true swarm of ducks, gulls and swans. The municipal authorities have complained about all the people feeding bread to the birds, but to no avail. Evidently it is a die-hard tradition.

My own incipient tradition of being on a date regularly can hardly be said to be harmful to either wildlife or myself, but after Sabine entered my life, I'd really like the whole project abandoned. It did not improve matters that I was about to meet with a woman this afternoon of whom I hardly had any impression.

When I was about to order a double espresso, I was tapped on my shoulder and to my surprise it was Elizabeth.

- What on earth ... Well, hello Elizabeth.

- Hello Christian. Can you order a latte for me, too?

As a bolt from the blue it dawned on me: Of course Elizabeth was Lizzy!

- You bandit, you! Haha. How could I fall for such an obvious stunt.

- I was actually convinced that you had guessed it was me. But I am so curious to hear about your project.

It was with a great relief that I could summarize the past week. Admittedly I had far from beaten Elizabeth's record number of dates, but I thought that the result until now was more than okay. I told her about my measly three dates, and that she herself was only number four in a row. It was clear that Elizabeth was disappointed with my pathetic efforts, but she listened attentively.

- In principle I am ready to bet on Sabine and drop the rest of the flock. Yes, I know it would be wrong, but she is just so lovely.

- I understand that, and can clearly see the lights in your eyes when you talk about her. Along the way, in my search earlier this year, I also had my problems, because it was so ingrained, perhaps even a reflex to fall in love with one person and immediately imagine how it could be a perfect relationship.

- Yes, I can remember some episodes ...

- Whether you choose to discontinue multiple dating is naturally your own choice, but I can recommend that you give yourself some more experiences.

- But do you think it will be fair to Sabine?

- She knows what she has agreed to from your descriptions. And she seems to be a sensible girl. Are you afraid of losing her already before you actually start a relationship, or what?

Again Elizabeth gave good food for thought. We've known each other for just over four months and I have great respect for her and the immediate and free-thinking quality that she brings to our conversations. As a woman, she is not overly solution-oriented, but rather inquisitive at examining alternative processes toward a target. This makes a perfect opponent for me because I often make spontaneous decisions without giving room for reflections.

- I really cannot promise you that I will continue to answer requests and go on more dates. Frankly, I can imagine that there will be more disappointments like those I told you about before.

- Nonsense. Do not be such a sissy.

- But you must accept if something else works for me or for men in general. Maybe I'm just in a phase that will pass.

- The stage is called fascination. It is just before love sets in and makes you blind!

She was right again. I could even feel how my description of Sabine was colored and influenced my original plan. At the same time, I was disenchanted with the meetings with Linda and Karla. It seemed absurd that there had been only three dates in total, when I went into this with expectations of a string of interesting and different women.

- Well then. I will not delete the profile. For now.

- Good! Find your inner fighter and never give up.

- This was just the kind of input I needed. I very much appreciate that you contacted me, Lizzy.

Elizabeth chuckled once again that she had tricked me. There is some truth here: I am about to enter the blind phase. Everything that Elizabeth had made me aware of was true.

The time was ripe to perform a mental search of my motivation, my actions and my general experience with women.

But I know myself well enough to realize it would be smarter to let my subconscious work a little further first. I needed a little distraction in order to focus on something else, so I went home to plow through some cookbooks, also in order to be inspired for Friday's gourmet meal. I would rather cook something relatively easy. Under no circumstances red meat. As much as I enjoy a good steak at a restaurant, I still have difficulties buying raw meat from a butcher. Furthermore, it can easily go wrong, especially if cooking is done in company with a very attractive girl, where my concentration is diverted too easily in the crucial minutes.

It will likely end up with fish and vegetables. Probably something in the oven, instead of a frying pan, because there the meal will cook by itself and I can focus properly on Sabine.

Wednesday 22nd September, 2010

Mental Searches

What an annoying day. New problems with a software solution, which I was sure we had tested all the way. No matter how confident one can feel about the logic of computers, there will apparently always be teasing details. Sometimes it may be an incorrectly placed comma or a missing parenthesis – and that is virtually impossible to find. Some years ago I found out why programmers tend to use copy/paste and not enter the code by hand. It is simply too risky to make a mistake and not even be aware of a simple typo. And these computers are some ungrateful beasts. They do exactly what you ask for, no guessing about the most logical, manmade errors.

The dialogue between the sexes is slightly similar. We tend to say one thing and think something else. Conversations between men can easily be understood immediatly, and probably the same goes among women. It's worse when a relationship enters the dangerous path where you think there is a common understanding through many long, rewarding and meaningful dialogues. Completely unprepared you sit there and are misunderstood or not understood at all.

A further complicating factor in this regard concerns the mix of reason and emotion. Not just rigorous logic, but a very dangerous cocktail of two rarely compatible elements. I'm now having an overdose of this exact cocktail and I only have myself to thank. My common sense says I must follow the advice of Elizabeth and continue to go on dates with several women. At the same side of the court is my stubbornness, pride and patience, a hard team up against the no less powerful emotions. Spontaneity coupled with a devil-may-care attitude, carried well on the way by an indescribable incentive to become one with Sabine. This is not pure lust either, because I need be more than the ordinary attraction before I think that way about a woman.

One-night stands never turned me on. The hassle of explaining there was no emotion in play, the inherent risk of hurting another human being, the brief pleasure and often lengthy consequence. Not my cup of tea at all.

Luckily there was a mail from Marie in response to my update on Friday. Her response lifted my mood a lot.

Dear Christian,
Thanks for your update.
I feel like quoting the Old Testament, from Proverbs: "Charm is deceitful and beauty is vain". You have been exposed to the essence when you met the incredible, alluring woman, I think. Just be glad that you quickly identified the facade and did not end up as one in the series of her conquests. As most proverbs go, it is not the entire truth, and you must not let yourself be deterred by a woman who had the looks but lacked the qualities you're looking for.
Several studies suggest that men live longer if they are with a younger woman, so you might be on track with Sabine. To my immense frustration the same studies show that the reverse is not true. I am rather delighted by younger guys, but in that constellation women, according to the researchers, do not get the same advantage of the age difference. The women who live longest, have partners of their own age. How can nature be capricious?

If you need professional lawyer help in the future, I have several good contacts, so just let me know. But it's best to avoid such needs.

Good luck with your ongoing project.

Love Marie

Oh yes, I can just imagine how she has torn her hair out when she read about those studies. She must have cursed scientists as well as nature and probably thought it must be individual, it only applies to the others, not to me.

There was a second mail. It was from Liva and lowered my mood a bit.

Hi Christian,

You might be surprised to hear from me after such a long time. But I need to cleanse my mind and even though I might not send this mail, it can work like therapy just to pretend I'm talking to you.

Frankly, things are not so well with Mick and me. After we got Xenia, he started to be more and more distant with his friends and he did not participate at home. I started to become unsure of whether he has an affair and am in two minds whether I should confront him with my thoughts. It's not like with you and I, we could always talk about everything, even when we broke up and afterwards. I am now in a new situation and afraid. Uncomfortable with my mistrust, uncomfortable with everyday life and simply sad. I know you can not do anything, and please do not perceive my mail as a cry for help. There is no violent conduct, rather absence. But that can be almost as hard to live with.

I have written and subsequently erased some other sections, but nevertheless choose to send this mail. Hope all is well in your life.

Hugs Liva

What the hell should I do?

Dear Liva,
Thank you for sending your mail.
You know I will always be there if you need help. I am glad
it is not about physical abuse (if so, I'd come by right away!).
But it hurts to read about your difficulties. It's so easy to
recommend you take a serious talk with Mick, but I would
rather offer that the two of us meet and have a talk. You are
welcome to suggest a time whenever it suits you. I will not
be pushy, but you can always count on support from here.
Loving greetings,
Christian

Darn. Tough for her. Fortunately Xenia is still so young that
she hopefully will not experience insecurity or lack of a
father figure, if this is a relatively new problem, which I
hope for Liva. I may get wiser, if I hear from her again.

Thursday 23rd September, 2010

A Trip on the MC

One of the joys of being the owner of a large motorcycle is the freedom to ride about on good roads in Denmark's glorious scenery. I've also been around in Sweden and further down in Europe, but today I was content to stay on Zealand. This could easily become the last journey of the season as one of the less pleasant experiences with an MC here in our climate is the inevitable pause to the fun because of winter.

When I got home, I was cold to the bones, and only thanks to a long stay in my Jacuzzi am I able to control my fingers on the keyboard. However, it was all worth it.

On the trip up past the Bellevue beach I recalled memories of the many summers I spent there with cute girls and sometimes just alone, but in precisely those cases with undisguised visual enjoyment of even more women. There were a number of years in which the artificial breasts stole too much attention, but in some ways that was festive enough. In recent years the trend has diverted from both silicone and topless bathing, and I appreciate that a bikini can highlight more than the previous liberality allowed. But it is a little annoying that so many months will pass before the beaches again invite you to a visit among the scantily clad chicks.

When I passed Louisiana, the Museum of Modern Art, I had to laugh a little about all the times I have pulled a new girlfriend in there just to find out she had no interest in – or understanding of – art. Without being decidedly art wise, I have both a passion of seeing beautiful things and also a certain curiosity to see the fantastic exhibitions. But visiting the place with a companion, who obviously would rather be somewhere else, that is a waste of time. Recently, I have been there alone, but maybe it's an idea to bring up with Sabine?

At the port of Elsinore, I had a short pit stop. More good memories of once I impulsively took the ferry over to Sweden with a girlfriend. We had just been on an early day trip, but ended up eating a delicious lunch north of Malmo, before we gunned southward to head back to Denmark over the uresund Bridge. This kind of spontaneous action is what makes life worth living. My thoughts went back to my dilemma and talk with Elizabeth yesterday. Should I be impulsive or reflect a little more about my options?

When you are in Elsinore in late September, the easiest solution is to head west and let the wind and the road form the basis for some meditation, so I drove on along the north coast.

Hornbaek beach in the fall is more dramatic than on lazy summer days. The sea shows a rugged strength, and the waves have white, aggressive tops. There weren't many boaters at this time of year, but I spotted some people walking their dogs farther along the shore. An experience like this is a real balsam for the soul - fresh air, freedom to do something unplanned and not depend on anyone. In return, nor someone to share experiences with. Dilemma deluxe reared its face again, and I drove on.

When I reached Raageleje, the temperature finally made me reverse my course back toward Copenhagen. Even with the leather suit in addition to several layers of shirts and sweaters, I began to yearn for a long, hot bath. I may have been speeding a bit toward the nearest highway and headed back into the garage here at Carl Johans Gade.

I almost fell asleep to the muffled sounds of my Jacuzzi. Numb in the body and even more in the mind of all the thoughts, this past week has brought. Yes, I would prefer to travel on tour with someone to share the joy. Yes, I would prefer to enjoy relaxing in the hot water with a beautiful woman. Yes, I would like to follow up on my plan to find not just one but several new women in my life. But I am also well underway, am I not?

Dizzy from all the fresh air, the warm bath and possibly influenced by the lack of lunch and a couple of glasses of wine as an accompaniment to the bath, I sat down to check the new responses to my online profile. There is an incredible number of desperate housewives out there. Taught by two-thirds of my handful of dates, namely Linda and Karla, and obsessed with my appointment with Sabine tomorrow I chose to ignore, or at least postpone response to new replies.

Of the incoming messages on my regular mail, I could see that the coding problem had been resolved. Tested thoroughly and in all likelihood no longer any cause for concern. That is until the next error appears. No, I really must regain my positive self and maintain my self-confidence!

Sabine had said something about self-confidence? Something about dreams? That the flying dreams were signs of ambition and self-confidence or something like that? I should perhaps try to be a little more attentive when falling asleep soon. It could be fun to tell her about an ultra experience tomorrow. I miss her already, and it dawns on me that it is only a week ago, I saw her for the first time. Well. Skip to next in-box mail.

It's from Daniel, who invites me to a round of beers marking his birthday on Tuesday. I can see in my calendar, that on the same afternoon there's an information session in one of my mutual funds, but with a little luck I can do both. A few of the core group usually remains over beer even after three hours of enjoying the hop among friends... It's too long ago since I've seen Daniel, Kasper and Mikkel. A threesome I have now known for a good ten years. We meet relatively frequently, but sometimes well over a month can pass without any contact. I wonder whether Laura is also invited, because it is now several years ago that Daniel and she broke up. This reminds me, too, that Laura knows about my project ... We chatted about it a while ago.

Daniel will get a confirmation in the mail immediately, and at the same occasion I will write a short update to Laura, where I can discreetly ask if she also pops up on Tuesday. I hope so, because her attendance decreases the geeky talk. Moreover, it will be easier to introduce the guys to my project if it surfaces through a talk with Laura in their company.

Not that I have high expectations on input from their side, but in a few days I will at least have a little more to tell them about Sabine. And tomorrow, I am to see her again! This time, the joy of expectation will hopefully not be the greatest.

Friday 24th September, 2010

A Romantic Dinner

Another day spent working from home – there are certain advantages to being your own boss. There is also a good side effect to having an exciting woman visit for dinner, my entire penthouse has been subjected to a very thorough cleaning. I have cleaned all the windows and even arranged fresh flowers, which only happens very rarely. I skipped buying plants, however, because they require too much care that I never get around to. But an extra handful of roses came in handy, so I can sprinkle rose petals on top of a filled Jacuzzi if I can lure Sabine into a bath during the evening.

The large bathroom is not just in pristine condition but also lined up with scented candles, and I've found new bath salts and oils. There are a couple of newly washed silk kimonos plus a pair of terry bathrobes, so she can choose to her own preference. I wonder a bit whether it will be inappropriate to show her around. Might seem presumptuous, or at least quite revealing, if I follow her from room to room, and she sees where the signals are pointing to. It is better if she discovers it outside my company, so she can calmly decide what she wants.

Midway through the preparations, I needed a break and checked my online dating profile and ordinary mail. There are still some visitors, but there is a decline in new replies. I could of course put it into hibernation. No, that would be wrong. Elizabeth would never forgive me, and my own stubbornness wins over the impulse. Besides, it is still entertaining to read the few incoming messages, but none today encouraged me to answer.

But a nice mail from William did. He wrote me about a somewhat different kind of burger restaurant we should try out. Far from McDonald's and the sometimes overly uniform café burgers. This concept was about producing the original burger of only the very best ingredients.

We have previously tested out new concepts in the Copenhagen restaurant arena, and although we only see each other months apart, it's always a pleasure to spend a few hours over a good meal with him. Our lives have evolved as differently as possible both regarding relationships and on the professional sides of life. Shortly after high school, William started dating his sweetheart, Janet, from one of our classes, and they have been married for an eternity. Two adult children, big house (though neither Volvo nor dog). But overall, they are the epitome of a loving, caring and traditional family. He has even kept the same job he landed after obtaining his engineering degree. His middle name could be Stable. I have no impression that he is bored in life, there are often long journeys associated with his job, and he has also traveled frequently with his family during all the years.

It will be good to see him again on Monday for burgers and some great beer, so I quickly replied to his mail with a confirmation. Wonder how he will react when he hears about me getting involving with a girl who technically could be the daughter to men of our age? Time will tell, and I still had to conquer Sabine more than was the case at this time.

The last part of the afternoon was spent preparing dinner. I had been in two minds about ingredients, but the choice fell on snapper and roughly chopped vegetables. Furthermore my home made sauce of sour cream, mustard, garlic and capers. Everything presented nicely in an ovenproof dish, and the hard work done, so we can start out enjoying a cool white wine. It seemed too exaggerated to start with champagne, but there are a couple of bottles ready for later. Those tiny bubbles fit exquisitely to the slightly larger ones in the bath. Or if that does not become a reality, they can be served in the sofa.

Despite the season I also prepared a classic tomato-mozzarella salad with fresh basil, doused with olive oil and balsamic vinegar. A freshly baked bread from Emmery's and we should be all set.

With an hour to spare before Sabine was expected to arrive, I checked the mail again and saw a new one from Liva.

Dear Christian,
Thanks for your support. I am glad, too, that I chose to send my first mail and it is reassuring to know you are still there. My life is like a vacuum and it is only my responsibility for Xenia keeping me sane. But I could almost equally well be alone with her, and this was not the intention on my part. I miss being able to talk with my boyfriend, I miss input from other adults in general. I have met some other mothers on the playground, but it is not the place for deeper conversations. My colleagues are still too young to contribute on relevant topics when we talk. I am becoming tired of hearing about their festive weekends.
Can we meet on Friday next week?
Love
Liva

It was impossible to fight against the emotions, and I got a sinking feeling of concern about her problem. It could also be due to hunger, but I was worried when I thought about the matter. Liva is a good person, extremely talented at her job and deserves better than an isolated existence. Of course I would be there for a chat.

Dear Liva,
Next Friday is fine with me. How about a cup of mocha at the French Café, around 4PM, by that time it's not too crowded. If you can leave your office a little early, we will probably have an hour before you need to pick up Xenia, I think.
Courage my good friend!
Sincerely,
Christian

One hour is better than nothing, and I hope it suits her. She has to bring Xenia home anyway and she didn't mention dinner, so I expect everything falls into place as I have proposed. There are also some ulterior motives in the fact that I could be lucky and have arranged a new Friday evening with Sabine, so it's best to keep the evening after 5PM vacant.

Right now she could be right around the corner, so it is appropriate to open a bottle and take one last tour of the apartment to ensure all details are ready for a hopefully great experience. My thoughts about Liva quietly disappear with the anticipation and joy of getting to spend a lot of hours with Sabine.

Monday 27th September, 2010

A Traditional Family

The burger restaurant is located close to my office, so I stroll off late afternoon to meet with William. He sent me a text message earlier and recommended that we should meet already at 6PM because you cannot reserve a table. There is a better chance to be served without delay if we start a little early.

On the way there I smile inside, and occasionally also externally, by the memories of my evening with Sabine Friday. We sat down with white wine in the living room, while dinner was in the oven, and luckily she liked my little appetizer consisting of salted crackers with hummus.

- You really have a nice apartment. What do you use all the space for?

- Well. I actually don't use most of the rooms. A couple of them are completely empty, and in some I just store things I don't use so often.

- Hmm, I certainly don't have that problem. My room is twenty square meters.

- And you have access to kitchen and bath?

- Certainly, but several times a week I visit the public swimming pool nearby. They even have a sauna.

I enjoyed seeing how relaxed and natural she was in my sofa. She fit pretty well there in the corner with her legs pulled up and her glass in hand. She wore a tight black t-shirt and very ordinary, blue jeans. Apart from a little discreet mascara there was no need for makeup or jewelry. She radiated a genuine and internal beauty and she was clearly aware of it.

Over dinner, she stunned me with a huge appetite and I was glad that I had used one of the bigger dishes, which she emptied at her third serving.

- Where does all the food go? You're so slim and please do not perceive my amazement as criticism. I'm just surprised and glad to see you like the meal.

- Hahah. I have this idea that my metabolism eats six times a day, but I only have four meals. And your mix of fish and vegetables is not heavy, but it tastes heavenly.

- For once, I can not say there is more to be served. But I can probably find something sweet for dessert.

- No, no. that is not necessary. I am completely satisfied regarding solid foods.

Aha. A hint, maybe even an invitation. If I play my cards right, perhaps dessert turns out satisfying a completely different hunger?

While I washed the dishes, Sabine visited the large bathroom, and to my delight the impression had worked.

- Oh, how wonderful. You have a Jacuzzi. That is even better than a sauna!

- Yes, it's nice after a long day at the office. How about I open a bottle of champagne and fill up with some other bubbles out there?

- That sounds pretty appealing, I think.

She smiled as she walked over to look through my music collection. She got some extra points in my gradebook when I heard from the bathroom that she had put on an album with Fourplay. Perfect choice!

For some inexplicable reason, but probably because of her natural being, it seemed quite normal that we got ready to enjoy the small and large bubbles together. Her body was exactly as I had imagined. Not that the tight t-shirt had hidden much, but it was a pleasure to see her without it. Her legs were sufficiently muscular and despite the hefty meal her stomach was almost flat.

How did she do it? In a brief moment I was anxious whether she could be anorexic, but her figure did not imply anything along those lines.

- Say - ehm, are you going to bring beers too? She asked with a smile.

- ...? What do you mean?

- Well, you're bringing a six pack ... Beautiful belly!

- Hahaha. You are good at compliments and thank you. I was just admiring your belly which shows no sign of our solid meal.

It seems that we both passed the requirements for admission to each other. When we later arrived in the bedroom, the temperature rose several degrees and I cannot remember when we finally fell asleep.

There was much to rejoice, while I found my way to the rendevouz with William, and before I knew it, I was in front of Halifax, the burger restaurant. He stood at the bar and was waiting with a draft beer.

- Hey Christian, we are in line for the next table. Good to see you, which kind of beer would you like?

As always William was in a good mood. And we were both hungry, so when we sat down to study the menu, we agreed on two big Lone Star bandits. Fries as side order for one a mixed salad for the other. That way we could cover all needs and tastes.

- You look extremely happy, what happened?

- Well, I've met a girl who is absolutely fantastic.

- Thought so. It had to be something like that. Do tell!

- Her name is Sabine, she's studying media sciences and I love the taste of her.

- HA! Ok, you don't need to get into that kind of detail. And how did you meet her?

- Long story. I created a profile on online dating. The short version is that she replied and we've seen each other a few times over the last week. Latest this Friday, where she stayed overnight.

- Well, I'll be darned.

- Yes, it comes as a surprise to me too, but she is so totally wonderful.

- So then, you've been with her the entire weekend?

- No, I haven't. Hehe. For the first time in history, I woke up and discovered that the girl had sneaked out without me noticing it. But we fell asleep quite late.

- Did she run out on you, you poor thing?

- I don't think so. She mentioned going for a visit to her uncle, who lives on an island. Nekseloe, I think. But she had written a sweet greeting on the mirror in the bathroom.

- With lipstick like in another b-movie?

- No, much more refined. It was not until I went into the steam bath a 'thank youĒ was revealed with a heart and a smiley at the mirror. She is astute.

When I woke up alone Saturday morning, I was initially disappointed that Sabine had stolen away, but she had been talking about her weekend plans over dinner, so I was a little prepared, after all. I looked in the kitchen and living room for a message in the belief that she had left a greeting. Only after I had my bath did I see the sweet greeting on the mirror, and I was calm again.

- We have exchanged a few text messages over the weekend and will meet again on Thursday. But of course, her days are busy with studying.

- She sounds like a good match for you. You also have your need for time by yourself, so I can only say good luck – and congratulations on the catch.

Finally a positive response from one of my friends. To be fair, William had not received the full history about my search for three women, but he was not afraid to share in my joy over the new twist, my life had taken. Maybe it was easier to assess a potential new girlfriend after fairly ordinary circumstances, than the entire project to search for three different women?

It will be fun to hear comments from the other guys and possibly Laura, when we meet tomorrow evening to celebrate Daniel's birthday.

Tuesday 28th September, 2010

Boys' Night Out

I showed up to celebrate Daniel at the agreed pub around half past seven after a long afternoon with good advice on investments. As expected, the hard core drinkers remained, comprising birthday boy Daniel, and in addition Kasper, Mikkel and to my great joy also Laura, Daniel's ex. They had been drinking for some hours, so they were all in a good mood.

- Congratulations and cheers.

- So, did you become any wiser regarding finances?

- Well, they mostly advised on what to stay away from - they still dare not recommend specific projects, I think.

- Speaking of projects, how are things with your dates?

Laura had not forgotten our chat several days ago.

- What?

The outbreak came in a chorus from the guys as the three tenors, and we all laughed at their synchronous reaction. But I knew very well that they were surprised. They know my past life style in which I have often expressed my satisfaction about being single.

Apart from Mikkel we have all been through close relationships, which in various ways were interrupted and we had haphazardly tried to comfort each other when things went wrong. Mikkel is and remains a workaholic, and he seems to be happy without a permanent girlfriend. Kasper had a failed relationship quite a long time ago and has since also devoted himself to his work. After Daniel and Laura broke up, all five of us, as the singles we were, enjoyed various festivities together. Sometimes a New Year celebration, sometimes a mid-summer picnic.

- Well, it all started a month ago when I created an online profile and searched for three different women.

- Hardly needed for cleaning, dishwashing and laundry, said Kasper in his usual good-natured teasing way, because in this crowd I'm also known as something of a freak in terms of being meticulous, especially with my apartment.

- Hehe. No, not exactly. I wanted an exotic, a soulmate and a fresh, maybe a little wild-at-heart.

- How did you select those qualities? Daniel asked.

- Easily. I considered the basic types that I am attracted to. But the first two are hard to combine, and my curiosity requires the third. So eventually I became aware of the need for all three.

- As I asked before, how's it going? Laura asked.

- To be quite honest, I have been in doubt about the project's further development. Because I have met a girl who is so beautiful that I am ready to drop the further search.

- That's unlike you. Where's your patience?

- Tell us more about your new girl. What's she doing, how old is she?

- She's studying and ... she is twenty-eight. Her name is Sabine.

To my own amazement, I was a little ashamed that she was so young, but they accepted it nicely, although there were some envious glances from Daniel and Kasper.

I was very conscious not to talk in detail about all the properties of Sabine, I was fascinated by. We had only known each other for a very short time and were not officially a couple, but it was a pleasure to feel the inner joy just by talking about her. As far as I could interpret from my friends' reactions, they were most of all happy on my behalf, and I realized that there was no reason to be embarrassed anyway. After all, I would probably not be shocked or offended if one of the others found a girlfriend who was under thirty. Except perhaps if Laura found herself as a young guy. Oddly enough there are still some reservations when it comes to age difference that way.

When my phone suddenly rang and I saw that it was Sabine's number, I went outside and became the victim of friendly bullying by their somewhat obscene comments. But they were all curious, when I came back after a few minutes.

- So, she couldn't do without you anymore?

- Why doesn't she come by and have a drink with us?

- No, she is in the middle of an assignment, but we will be meeting again tomorrow. Don't worry. I hope this works out, and you will definitely get to meet her.

A few hours later, as I walked back home, it was with a pleasant peace of mind at how nicely they had all accepted this change in my attitude. Their first comments about my long period as a happy single had gradually been replaced by encouragement and advice. Mikkel in particular mentioned that it was probably healthy for me to get some new experiences. It would not surprise me if he even got a little inspiration to expand his own horizon.

Most of all, it was nice to once again feel the joy of expectations in looking forward to an evening in the company of my so-called new experience. Although I have an appointment to visit Ulrich tomorrow afternoon, I can easily make it home for the evening.

Whether Ulrich tomorrow lets me talk more about this whole development, or the conversation will be derailed again, time will tell. Now at least I got really positive feedback from the guys and Laura, and overall it has been a nice celebration of Daniel, even without gifts and cakes.

Wednesday 29th September, 2010

Mail From the Ex

For the first time in many years, I do not look forward to going to bed and have the entire mattress to myself. Sabine has opted to go home, according to her quite plausible explanation that she has to get up very early tomorrow. My apartment seems empty and deserted, differently so than just one month ago. During the past years I have enjoyed resting in my own company and liked that there were no commitments or others to take into account.

Now I sit here with the scent of a young, beautiful woman in every deep breath and just wish that I could wake up next to her tomorrow. Strange how life can be changed at short notice.

I had no complaints about the evening, quite the contrary. There had been not time for either a romantic dinner or rose petals in the bath, but we favored our hunger for each other in the living room pretty soon after her arrival. Our shared need to explore more physical details were at the same level, and for my part, these reciprocal studies could very well last some time yet.

There is something special about the freshness in body and energy, a young girl possesses. When that is integrated with the immediate closeness, we also experience by psychological wavelength, I have no other demands of life.

As we rested comfortably close and exhausted on the sofa and shared a huge bottle of water, she asked a little about my past life. I told her about my marriage with Liva. About how it started a with few years of flirting and curiously enough, was completed by about two years as lovers again after we were legally divorced. Without too much detail, I mentioned the fact that I still have a great respect for Liva, but she is now a mother with her new boyfriend, and as a result we are not seeing each other very often. I wondered whether it was appropriate to bring up the latest news and decided to disclose that I was to meet Liva over coffee on Friday. To my undivided joy Sabine reacted positively and praised me on being a support to my ex-wife, when the need arose for a little encouragement. It could just as easily have gone the other way, but as far as I can interpret, there is no jealousy to track. And it's a great relief to have brought it up, so I don't need to conceal anything or think up white lies. We even agreed to meet again Friday night, after my appointment with Liva, and I am happy that we have found a rhythm that suits us both so soon. The mysterious discomfort, I sometimes experience when missing her – for instance now, that she has chosen to sleep at home in her room – is something I will probably have to deal with at one point or another. But up till now, I cannot help but be extremely proud of the achievements of my project.

After Sabine had heard of Liva, I wanted to hear a little more about her own experience with relationships. She has obviously had some boyfriends, but none of longer durations. Before she spent her years in South America, there had mostly been ordinary sweethearts from school, and because of the near-vagabond-like life later on, it had been impossible to build solid relationships. Maybe it's to my advantage that she can now look forward to at least three to five years of stability? In any case I will do what I can to ensure she stays, and preferably not only in her studies but also as a more durable part of my life. Her scent is simply not enough.

Earlier in the day I visited Ulrich and got further insight into how a broken family (with children) has its very own challenges. Among the positive changes I could see that there is much more order in the house. Ulrich has apparently been right in his assumptions that his tidiness was sabotaged somewhat by Karen, soon legally his ex. It must be easier for him to keep order in the house when he only has the children every other week, and in relation to my own home there is still a world of difference. But it's probably unfair to compare when my home usually consists of only one person for whom to cook, clean and do the laundry.

I have sometimes wondered when visiting some of my single friends. Their homes can at times be more messy and indeed dirty, than in a family with three children. But as noticed, Ulrich's house was nice today.

There was a much better mood than in the past where he and Karen struggled to get the marriage working. Even on good days, it had been obvious that there was a lot smoldering under the surface. But historically, many marriages probably survived periods of problems, and in some cases benefit all parties in the end. Ulrich and I have had many conversations about that, but as things evolved, I am pleased on his behalf at the final break.

Of course it has consequences in everyday life, both for the children and for the adults. His eldest daughter grumbled, that she could not find the drinking glasses when she was at her mother's and when she was at home with dad, there were no glasses because mother had taken them. It will never be the same again as when they were a family with all that entails.

I stick to my own choice of not wanting to have children. If Liva and I had had one or more kids, we might have stayed together, but when I look at Ulrich's life now, that's no guarantee. It's more like a reason to delay a nasty decision, which could have been done quickly, though not painlessly. There will always be pain when you interrupt a relationship. In a way you can be sure of getting hurt already in the same second, you fall in love. I ought to know now, and I should also think a little bit more about what I've started with Sabine.

As expected I didn't get a chance to discuss my situation with Ulrich. It requires a little more calm and slightly fewer children requiring attention. However, the visit gave me food for thought, particularly about my willingness to seriously get into a relationship with Sabine. Emotion and reason are incompatible. Again.

I could spend all night philosophizing, but decide to check my mail one last time before I head for my suddenly empty bed.

Dear Christian,
A cup of coffee at the French Café tomorrow sounds fine. I can be there at 4PM, and Xenia just needs to be picked up before 5:30, so I am looking forward to an hour with a guarantee of good talking.
Thanks again for being there – it means a lot to me, but I am sure you already know.
Hugs Liva

Thursday 30th September, 2010

Status

To slightly paraphrase an old bon-mot, I can safely say that this is the last day of the first month of my project. I want three new women in my life and I choose to go for an exotic type, a soul mate and a fresh, maybe a little wild-at-heart. The latter mostly because I know myself well enough to realize I need new input at regular intervals.

One day long ago I spoke with a motorcyclist out at Langelinie, where people with a passion for these beautiful vehicles often meet during the summer months. He said that every enthusiast should have not one but three motorcycles: A Harley for the short-cruise tours from one café to the next. An off-road bike for trips out into the wilderness, so you can get away from the roads. And finally a racing bike when the need arises for speed and excitement. I can easily agree with this philosophy, but eventually my choice fell on a touring bike. Had I been living in a country with more friendly taxation and not least a warmer climate, I'd definitely like to have permanent ownership of the other kinds – among them certainly a Ducati as the icing on the cake – but I am more than satisfied with my Diversion 900.

It would probably have created more response from my friends, if my project had focused about buying some more bikes. I reflect on my talks with Robert and Ulrich which didn't result in useful feedback. That's not surprising, because both are in critical situations regarding relationships. Robert is once more on an undefined break and Ulrich is well underway in the phase of separation before the final divorce after too many years of trying to save his marriage.

I had received more input when exchanging emails with Marie. Unostentatious as always but with a little advice from a female angle. Sometimes it may be easier to exchange written communication when issues affect emotions and decisions. You are not so easily disrupted, and thoughts can flow freely flow from one party at a time. The fact that she is a thoughtful woman just adds fuel to the dialogue, and it will be fun to keep her updated in the near future.

Nikolai's comment that I would be risking a lot of hassle has made me think a great deal these last few weeks. However, the worst trouble has been to filter out dull responses to my profile. And then there was the awful date with the lawyer, Linda. But I learned one important thing: to avoid too much research before I meet a new woman. The very exotic Karla had started many fantasies in my mind, both before we met and during the first part of our meeting. And even if I had done research on her in advance, I would hardly have found out that she considered both adultery and lying as her hobbies. I can only look back on the experience as an unexpected humorous chapter and an additional self-insight. I do not necessarily need to be the one and only for a woman with whom I have an affair or a relationship, but I draw the line if she is married. To me, marriage means that you promise each other eternal fidelity.

When it comes to Benjamin, I could just as well have proclaimed that I was looking for a new motorcycle. He likes four wheels and I like two. He is in a marriage where the most important part is getting practical needs satisfied, and I'm looking for something else. At least he wished me good luck and was in no way condemning. And I guess that next time we meet, the conversation will be more about politics than relationships.

When Lizzy proved to be Elizabeth, it dawned on me that I'm having some of the same dilemmas that she had experienced previously - the recurrent idea of that special someone. Perhaps it is in our genes, after so many hundreds of years following the same model. I must really try to keep my focus and not bow in to the urge to be with Sabine all the time. It's tough when I am simultaneously so fascinated by her beautiful mind – and her body!

As for William, it was a little unfair to compare his reaction to all the others. He hadn't got the whole story about three women. My obvious happiness from having just spent the previous evening with Sabine revealed me and everything I talked about was focused on her. I imagine that he would accept my crazy plan if he knew about it. He is the epitome of a good support no matter what.

The trio consisting of Daniel, Kasper and Mikkel had teased me, but mostly they were curious about the project in general and Sabine in particular. It would not surprise me if they and even Laura enter into a bet that I am single again within a year. As for myself, I have no idea where this leads me to.

The best things in life right now are the warm feelings activated by simply knowing Sabine exist. Being able to generate such intense emotions is like an aphrodisiac, but there are also side effects. The idea of losing Sabine lies just below the surface in spite of my staunch commitment to be careful. I shouldn't proceed too quickly and I must be cautious in my progress. In any event, we have not come to anything like a shared daily life, so it is best to simply enjoy the certainty that I will see her again tomorrow.

My appointment with Liva tomorrow afternoon gets me on a totally different track. I wonder how bad things are with her boyfriend, Mick. Could he be on his way out of his obligation as a father? It has happened before, couples breaking up soon after they become parents. But their daughter must be nearly three years old by now, so it's a surprise to me if their problem began recently. It could also have been a gradual slide, or maybe Liva has been trying to save it all for some time, as was the case with Ulrich.

I will certainly offer my sympathy to her story. I'll try not to give too much advice and listen more than talk. It can also serve as an injection of realism to me, which certainly won't do any harm. Wasn't it the Romans, who said something like 'Memento mori – remember your mortalityĒ to their most talented fighters, so they should not be blinded by their own success?

In my case it should be called 'Remember you can only trust yourself.' Nevertheless, I am also aware that I cannot always trust myself. My struggle is between the impulsive and spontaneous, that is, feelings, versus the annoying knowledge and subsequent load of experience on how much it hurts to lose someone.

However, it would be a poor and boring life, if there wasn't room for a little of everything, and my conclusion at September's events is fixed. I would not do anything differently, and I am excited as a child before Christmas!

October

Friday 1st October, 2010

A Big Decision

It was both pleasant and sad to see Liva again. The feeling of security that we had built up through our marriage, has always left us with a special closeness to each other. I have a built-in loyalty and craving to protect her, which has survived the difficult time following our break. When she later became Mick's girlfriend and mother of their daughter, I thought that maybe we could have saved our relationship with a child. Her reliance on my company could have been replaced by the task of being a mother, and I would also have been given new input. Unfortunately, couples all too often go for that solution and wind up some years later with even greater difficulties. It was better to be happy on her behalf.

My emotions were in uproar when she began to tell about her everyday life with Mick, because it proved to be worse than I had imagined.

- He spends all his time with his friends. They even take off in the weekends and I might just as well be a single mother.

- Do you know what they're doing, where do they go?

- He doesn't say much. Fishing trips, sometimes, or to a cottage in the countryside.

- Do you think he has a mistress, and that he is lying to you?

- The thought has occurred to me, but no. If that were the case, he would not come home dirty and greasy, so it's probably friends.

- For how long has this been going on?

- Well, it has escalated the past six months. In the beginning it was just a couple of times a month, but now I barely see him.

Liva has always been rather dependent on a secure base. When we were together, it was always important for her to know when I came home and where I was. But I also thought it was natural to coordinate with each others' chores and got used to it. Mick could obviously do not accept the same rules.

- Have you tried to call him when he is away for a weekend?

- His phone is usually switched off or out of reach. And then he says it ran out of battery when he finally comes home.

- Well, those things happen. But I can understand you feel abandoned.

- I just get so lonely. There is no one to talk to, and it is just plain wrong.

It was not easy to cheer her up. What could I do? Hire a private detective to spy on Mick seemed like a bad movie. It was probably best to just put an empathetic ear to her stories. If it was good company she missed, I could show compassion now and then, and be an intellectual partner to her. Elizabeth needed that too, so it's perhaps a general need for women.

- You can call me anytime. We still communicate well and please tell me if there is something I can do for you.

- Thanks, it has helped already. I have to pick up Xenia now, so thanks for showing up on such short notice.

We walked together toward the Triangle, where she was catching a bus. From my side it was a pure reflex to kiss her goodbye but then she gave me a long hug, and fortunately the situation was not awkward. It can often be difficult to interpret the boundaries, and whether the signals are deciphered wrongly in these circumstances. She hadn't even heard about my life, so she surely thought that I was still single. Technically, I suppose I am, but our meeting had also spawned memories about being two in everyday life. We had some great years together back then.

All this combined with my recent thoughts when Sabine chose to go home instead of staying overnight, brought out my inner devil of impulse. Life is too short to wait and see. On the short walk home, I reached a resolution that gives me a new challenge tonight. I will suggest to Sabine that she moves from her rented room and into my apartment. She can even get her own room and peace to study if she wants. We need not be together constantly, because she is at the university and I am usually in the office most days. But knowing she is there and knowing she belongs, that feels right.

How should I phrase it, though? She has done some spontaneous things in her life, so I guess that she will at least consider my offer. It should preferably not seem too desperate from my side, we have not even known each other for a month. But it is not a marriage proposal either. I can present it as a practical arrangement, where she saves her rent? How unromantic. No, of course I will not be afraid to say I'm in love with her. We have not yet said the dangerous three words, but tonight I'm ready. I have to listen to my inner fighter.

It is a good thing that I always keep champagne in stock, because tonight may soon become one of the bigger events. Is there a risk that she gets scared by my suggestion? Should I quietly get into the topic, or just be straightforward? What if she declines? Why should she ... We enjoy each other's company and I deprive her no freedom. We can continue our parallel lives but with a shared base. The actual moving can be done quickly, because she has so few belongings, and a couple of my guest rooms are already furnished better than where she lives now. It should be possible to persuade her. How can she say no to me?

I will make sure there are candles lit all over the place when she comes over. The food will be in the oven, and when we sit down with a drink, it will make or break. Once I have come to a decision, I have to act, possibly because I may also be in doubt and toss and turn for and against. Just like before jumping into cold sea water on an early spring day, it is sometimes best to disconnect from the brain and simply jump into it. Oddly enough, I had not imagined that the meeting with Liva would have this impact, but I send her a warm thought and hope that she gets a grip on her problems before they grow over her head. Mick really is a fool, and Liva still is a very beautiful woman!

Monday 4th October, 2010

An Easy Move

Relocation is not at the top of my favorite tasks. I'd rather do without all the hassle of packing things into boxes without getting them too heavy and having to make decisions on whether to throw stuff away or save it. When Liva moved, I was happy to keep the apartment and even achieve the positive side effect of reducing my belongings. If and when a friend needs help moving I can step in, and it has happened a few times, too, that my back and thighs have hurt a full week after forcing long stairs with a myriad of moving boxes.

Sabine's relocation struck a record at the opposite end of the scale. It was only the two of us, but everything was over and done in half a morning and could almost be compared to packing for a trip. Clothes, books and some bags. And shoes, of course – the stock of shoes in my apartment has multiplied, but there is plenty of room in the closets inside her room. I insisted that she should get one of the corner rooms so she can study in privacy when the need for concentrated reading arises. In return, she stood firm that we should buy some plants, also for the living room, and I must admit, it creates a little more cozy atmosphere.

Her lease ran on a weekly basis so both practically and financially, this was the absolute easiest relocation I had ever been part of. Three times up the lift and few hours to arrange clothes in the cupboards. The rest of Saturday was spent shopping, including trips to various flower shops and as we finally cooked dinner together, I felt happiness spreading throughout my body.

- I am so glad that you agreed to this.

- Had you been nervous about it?

- I didn't even have time for that. To be quite honest, it was a whim I got Friday late afternoon.

- While you had coffee with Liva?

- No, but soon after. I was reminded of all the benefits of being two in everyday life.

I talked briefly about Liva's problems and could see that Sabine sympathized. There were no signs of jealousy, which made me even more happy. I have really been lucky here. It might be true that I find myself in a phase of blind trust that Sabine is perfect for me, but I will allow myself to enjoy every moment.

When I see her walk through the room or stand in the kitchen, I am repeatedly fascinated by her feminine grace. The way she moves with her back straight radiates a self-awareness, which appeals to me immensely. The biggest risk with her being a more regular part of my life in the future is that I will probably find it hard to concentrate when I work at home. But I must coordinate so that her days at the university and my days at home coincide. If this is my only compromise I am well off. After all, today here at the office, I have again been thinking mostly about her and enjoyed every second of distraction.

As a sort of delayed welcoming gift I plan to visit the ground floor of the Magasin store on my way home and buy some exquisite items for Sabine. I have noticed that her closet in the bathroom contains surprisingly few things. Most women I've known over the years have had at least twice as much. Perhaps it is because she has not yet begun to worry about wrinkles and cellulite? I agree that would be pretty absurd. But some luxury skin care and fragrance from Issey Miyake could be in order.

But should I just put it on the shelves or do I get it finely wrapped as a gift? There is always a danger that she will take it amiss, though I only think that she deserves the best. I'll take a chance, but I think wrapping and handing it over as a gift is best. If she finds it as a surprise in the bathroom, it seems more like an allusion, and that is by no means my intention. She smells wonderful already, so from my hand, it is more about giving her a little extravagance in everyday life.

At any rate it will be a pleasure to come home to her shortly. The mere idea that she has been sitting in my apartment studying all day, gives me an inner warmth. Although we have been together all weekend, I long to look deeply into her eyes and hold her close to me. Everything about her fits so well with me and during our long walk around the lakes yesterday afternoon, I also found out that our strides are completely in rhythm. When I commented on it, she laughed wonderfully, because she had realized that as well.

Altogether, there are many thing to look forward to in my new life with Sabine. Tomorrow evening Robert comes over for dinner, and he becomes the first of my friends to meet her. I'm curious to see his reaction, but he sounded positive on the phone when we made the arrangement. He has often been surprised that I chose my single life, and now he will finally be right that it is never too late. Whether his so-called break with Tina has become more permanent, and the roles thus for a moment are reversed, will also be interesting to find out. However, it may equally well be that they have gotten together again and we are in a week of their living apart. His solution to only spend half the time together seems a little strange, but if it works for them, then fine with me. I prefer, at least now with Sabine, that she is here all the time. That she belongs here and that we have a shared base.

The apartment is big enough for us to not get on each others' nerves by enforced proximity, and in addition I have a feeling that she could never get me to become irritated. Otherwise, I had probably been satisfied that she stayed at her rented room so close by. Robert's model may work for him, but not for me. After I visited him the last time, it also seemed that it didn't work out in the end for him. He is probably already looking for a replacement for Tina.

If I know him correctly, he will want to hear whether Sabine has some cute friends at the university. But he will probably be disappointed, because she has not yet been building special bonds with anyone from her classes. Neither guys nor girls.

Oh no, Robert. You have to hunt again. Maybe I will suggest to him that he goes online to create a dating profile. My search for three has now given me one that is top notch.

Tuesday 5th October, 2010

Dinner With a Friend

Robert and I got a couple of hours to ourselves after dinner. Sabine had a movie on her laptop, she needed to watch prior to some discussions about it at the university tomorrow. She chose to do so in my bedroom where she would be undisturbed.

- Wow. I knew that you were picky, but this time you really found yourself a fine catch!

- Hehe. When you first greeted her, the look on your face was priceless! But yes, I'm hit hard by Cupid's arrow. Actually by the entire artillery.

- Too bad that she doesn't have a lot of friends in the same caliber.

- Well, you'll probably find something through the Internet.

My thoughts had come true tonight. Already at the first glass of wine, before we even got seated, Robert showed a great interest in whether Sabine had hooked up with one or more fellow female students, perhaps in a reading group. He can be quite direct when he sees opportunities for new, young blood. At one point I was almost nervous that she would consider his visit as a third degree interrogation. It must be his long experience of charming himself into women that triggers his machine gun volley of questions. I can still remember the old days, how he would converse with girls we met in town. I was a little quieter then, also because it was often difficult to hold a conversation in the loud music of discotheques. Robert was totally indifferent to that, it was all about talking himself into a new finding. As he tended to emphasize, no one could remember anything the day after anyway. In all likelihood, he was right about that.

His talk with Sabine had passed freely and easily, and I enjoyed listening to Sabine's answers and just watching her as she engaged in the conversation. As we mentioned that it was through online dating we met, Robert admitted he had also jumped on that wagon. Or rather that he had reopened his hibernated profile. He must have known that things would end with Tina as he had kept it in a paused mode.

- One thing is certain. When I last had it activated, I had more sex than at any other time in my life.

- Is that all you can think of? And are you done with Tina?

- Don't worry, my friend. It is better to be caught in a good triangle than in a vicious circle. When I see how lucky you've been, it gives me hope and confidence.

- You did not answer the questions, your bandit.

- Well, how can I avoid thinking about sex when I've just had dinner with one of the finest specimens of the weaker sex? And Tina is history.

It is interesting to see so differently some of my friends can act when they end in a break. Whether they are being left or are the leaving party, there are no two identical stories about how to best move forward. Robert is very quick to jump on the horse again, because his basic rule forbids him to have a girlfriend who has reached the age of forty. It goes without saying that his relationships under these circumstances must end after a dozen years. He has always filled the gap between long relationships with a sea of single ladies. There's nothing wrong with his self confidence, and I sometimes envy him for his very direct approach to life. Yet I do not think it would work for me. Without going specifically in grief, I have in similar periods put my love life on stand-by and focused on other things. The few times in recent history where both Robert and I were hunting, he rapidly fell into his old role. And I would be standing there wondering if I was already losing my hearing as a grumpy old man.

Intelligent and challenging conversations should preferably be as tonight. I was quite surprised how much Robert knew about Sabine's studies. He has probably once had a go with someone else studying media sciences. I can still be confused about the sequence of Bachelor, Master and the other titles, she has the opportunity to build on her curriculum.

When Robert went home, I went to check if Sabine was still watching her movie, but she was adorning my bed like a sleeping princess. I wonder if she wakes up when I'm about to accompany her in a little while? It is the fourth night in succession she is here, and at one time sex life is bound to normalize, even for us. I wouldn't mind if she were in a deep sleep, I would just like to fall asleep listening to her breathing. But I also know that she can easily get me on to other thoughts, if she wakes up. I wonder if she will be offended if I do not wake her up? No, that is not her nature.

Fortunately, she was happy with my gift. It turned out that she had just temporarily run a little low in her stock of lotions and perfumes, so everything was much appreciated. She had complimented me earlier on my use of Issey Miyake and their new range for women is perfect for her own, natural and fresh fragrance. Originally it was Liva, who introduced me to the brand, but as with all perfumes and women, they form special and individual combinations, as long as they don't overdo it.

I don't think it is possible for me to get an overdose of Sabine. But I will be careful this time and not risk getting too much. It's just fine that she needs to be at school tomorrow so I can stay home. Perhaps it can also work if we both have days, where we work from the apartment, we'll figure that out. It seemed perfectly natural when she left Robert and me in the living room earlier and it didn't trigger any thoughts of antisocial behavior. Instead I value enormously when a girlfriend is able to occupy herself and I like that her studying keeps her busy.

Could it be a sign that she wants to be awakened, when she chose my bed? It is impossible to gauge, because she has not slept alone in his own room yet. The more I think about my little luxury dilemma, the more difficult it becomes to find a reasonable solution. I don't want to cause her sleeping late tomorrow. To me, it does not matter when I wake up, but she has lectures to attend to. I'm sure Robert never experienced this kind of anguish. But I prefer to consider things wisely, at least once in a while. At the end of the day, I often realize that the whole thing was just something that rummaged in my own head. Regardless, it's time to go to bed.

Wednesday 6th October, 2010

A New Life

I could have saved myself the concerns last night about causing Sabine to be late this morning. As she said on the way out the door, only slightly delayed, she is old enough to be responsible for her own time. When she woke me up a little before six o'clock with some gentle touches, I initially thought it was still in the middle of the night. A half hour later she went for a shower, and I fell asleep again briefly, grateful for life in general and for my professional freedom in particular. The second awakening consisted of kisses and a confirmation that she probably would arrive on time.

Of course I should take good care of her, but she is right in saying that I am not responsible for her life. She thought it was a little funny when I told her about all my thoughts of late last night. At one time I was a little nervous about whether she would perceive it as being overly protective. It seemed, however, rather as though she appreciated being respected, so I could stay in bed with extra good conscience and sleep another few hours after she left.

During summer I can easily get up before seven o'clock, but as autumn sneaks into the country and the sun is up later, I value a couple of hours more under the quilt tremendously. My running trip around the lakes is also more unobstructed when I can avoid the early joggers. Today my plan was to move forward with a description of a new business plan, but after I had eaten a late brunch, I started doing some cleaning instead. It is not because Sabine is untidy in any way, but the place messes up easier with two people at home. Or maybe it's because time passes with other things when she is here. I can readily imagine how a home with kids can be a nightmare to maintain. At least we have no toys thrown all over the place today.

These considerations led me to think of Nikolai, who currently spends his entire day fussing about Erica, his daughter of eighteen months. He is trapped in the mix of a long parental leave and an ungrateful job market, the poor guy. But having Erica only a few hours at the daycare around midday, it is hopeless to find time and energy to apply for new jobs. The mere challenge of meeting up for interviews with the uncertainty that Erica suddenly may need to be picked up makes Nikolai's situation difficult. It doesn't make his life easier that he has not been getting his full night's sleep for many months. I am better off when the main problem is a little more hair in the bathroom.

Early in the afternoon I sat at my computer partly to get going with a new business plan and partly to check my mail.

Hi Christian,
On Friday Rosa comes home early and takes care of Erica in the afternoon. I need to get out a little. Are you ready for some beer and dinner somewhere in Frederiksberg?
Hope you are well.
Nikolai

Hi Nikolai,
You won't believe this, but I was just thinking about you. All is really well here and I have a lot to tell, so let's meet at Berlin Bar at 5PM Friday. Look forward to some good news from here.
Christian

Funny that he had written to me almost in the same minute as when my cleaning made me think of the differences in his and my life. My concerns about responsibility on Sabine's behalf fade completely compared with his, spanning from understaffed institutions to various diseases infecting the children. I must certainly learn to be more relaxed and Nikolai is usually a good catalyst for that. He may also be a bit of a devil's advocate, because he points out things which could be problematic. But the effect on me is that I take it more easy and feel confident that things will resolve themselves.

For instance, he had recently warned me about dating a lot of women to find my three favorites. None of us had imagined back then, less than a month ago, that I would now find myself living with a young girl. He will struggle to find negative aspects of this new development, I think, except for some sarcastic comment that my overall project is not quite complete, since I failed to find all three. But life can play you so many wonderful cards. Once he meets Sabine, I am sure he will understand and respect my choice.

As a corollary, I might as well go delete my online dating profile. It would be unfair to Sabine if she accidentally found out that I'm still actively searching. And that was a good decision, because I could see that she had removed her own profile when I logged in.

Dear Elizabeth,
Thanks for the inspiration to start searching for three women. As you understood when we last met, I had been in doubt about the model. It has turned out that I have fallen in love with one of the women I met. Just like you experienced during your search, it seems that I fall back into traditional

patterns. When I told you about Sabine, I had only just met her but now she is living with me and I have deleted my online dating profile.

You advised me to continue the project, but it feels wrong. Maybe women are better at multitasking, as we so often joke about. Maybe I am still in the blind phase (I don't doubt that). But I am happy, and that is the most important part. I also look forward for you to meet Sabine.

Sincerely,

Christian

With a hint of bad conscience, I sent the mail off to Elizabeth. Her advice was for once ignored. There might be other men out there who are better at keeping many relationships running simultaneously, but when I cannot even imagine having to date a new woman, I am sure that it would be wrong to continue the project. Instead, I look forward to Sabine coming home and the fact that I have been given a whole new meaning to my life thanks to Elizabeth.

Thursday 7th October, 2010

Surprise

A big surprise awaited me when I came home from the office this evening. There was a pram outside my door next to the elevator. I have no neighbors because I live on the top floor, and I found it a bit mysterious if Sabine had a friend visiting. When I entered my apartment, I could hear voices from the kitchen and went directly out there.

Sabine and Liva were sharing bottle of red wine!

- Hello Christian, I was hoping you'd be working at home today but Sabine let me in.

- I hope that's OK, and you've told me a little about Liva's situation, so we've been waiting for you to come home.

I was mildly nonplussed. Sabine behaved like an ordinary lodger, and I guessed that she had not told Liva about the real context here.

- You never told me that you had sublet a room, when we had coffee last Friday?

- Ehm, no, I did not. There was so much other stuff to talk about.

- And now I totally regret that I had not phoned you in advance. But the thing is that I really need a pause with Mick. So I was hoping that I could stay here a while until I get a better grip on everything.

- It would be nice having a little more company, Sabine said. And Xenia is so sweet. She lies asleep on the sofa. But it's not my apartment, so it's up to you, Christian?

Maybe Sabine should consider studying drama instead of media sciences. Her tackling of the potentially critical situation deserved an Oscar. But I did not understand yet why she had chosen to appear as my lodger. Was it to protect Liva, who was already depressed? Was it to protect me, so I didn't need to explain the sudden development since last weekend? I thought it best to play along and question her at the earliest possible opportunity. And I had given my word to Liva to help where and if I could. The apartment is large enough and if it is just for a short while ...

- Well, we can probably figure something out. But what have you told Mick?

- He has left for a prolonged autumn holiday with some friends. I can't endure being at home anymore. When he comes home, this will teach him a lesson, if he even remembers me.

She was really upset and mad at him. But seen from Liva's viewpoint, it made sense. She escaped from being alone with all her thoughts and where else could she possibly go? If I could just get Sabine on a one-to-one, there was a chance I could get a better overview of the situation. As saved by the bell Liva offered to fetch a couple of pizzas as a token of thanks that she could stay here a while.

When she left, Sabine broke out in laughter. I could not help but laugh, too.

- Why on earth did not you tell her that we are lovers? Because you're not just a lodger here. Or have I misunderstood something?

- It all happened so suddenly. I quickly found out that she was Liva, and perhaps it is a kind of female loyalty, but I could not make myself tell her the truth. And after she had been here a bit, it seemed easier to pretend that I rent a room. And in a way, that is what I do.

- But not in that way! Are we to play an act facing my ex-wife, and in my own home?

- Let us just take it as it comes. It's somewhat entertaining, and I'll be visiting your bedroom. But you must admit that it would have been tough for Liva, if I had told her the whole truth.

- You crafty woman, you! I'm not entirely sure that this is smart. But I respect your thoughtfulness. At best, she will be out within a week.

Sabine smiled and winked seductively to me while she uncorked a new bottle. Could she conceivably have a strange fantasy about being the naughty maid in a home where she plays around with the husband? I can never be quite sure about women, but I never tire of their ingenuity.

After Liva came back with the take-out, we talked more about the practical details. As we each had our obligations with jobs and studying – and in Liva's case, a child in a nursery home – it would most likely work out fine. We agreed that there was no need to make detailed arrangements for meal times. Our respective programs for the morning would be coordinated, so there was no chaos where all of us had to leave simultaneously. Liva would be first out handing off Xenia for daycare. Sabine rarely had early lectures, so she'd be off next. I had gotten used to not be early on the pitch for a long time.

- But what about Xenia? She sleeps through the night, doesn't she?

There's nothing worse than a screaming baby...

- You can be quite calm. She doesn't suffer from colic or sleepless nights. I promise you that you will never even know she is here.

- Apart from diapers and a large vehicle out by the elevator.

They both laughed at my skepticism to having a baby here. But the decision was taken, and I'm still not quite sure how much I influenced the outcome. Now they have both gone to bed. Liva and Xenia have a room facing the street, and Sabine is in her own room for the first time, which feels very strange. She's just becoming an integral and valued part of my life, and then Liva comes along and changes everything.

If someone is up for a sleepless night, it will be me. I hope Sabine will visit my bedroom.

Friday 8th October, 2010

Will There Be Trouble?

- Say, have you gone completely mad?

Nikolai was well underway on his third beer, but as I had so much to tell, I was just about done with my second.

- I told you that I had news. But the latest twist has come unexpectedly, and a few days ago I was just super happy about Sabine.

- For how long do you expect to keep it a secret to Liva that Sabine is not just a lodger? And how do you think she will react?

- Well, I do not know. It's all so new to me. And it's not my fault, things just happened in strange order.

As Nikolai had first heard about Sabine's moving in, he was decidedly happy on my behalf and had almost praised me for the initiative. Relatively soon after that I had continued telling about the story from yesterday, and initially his jaws had dropped. I understand that it is a big mouthful for Nikolai, but when Sabine came into my bedroom a little after midnight, I quickly forgot that there had been an increase in population in my apartment again in less than a week. She is good at distracting from anything but herself.

This morning I woke up alone in my bed and it took me awhile before it actually dawned on me. The apartment was very quiet, so they were probably all on their way to nursery school, job and the university. But there were signs in the kitchen, there were two cups in the sink and something resembling porridge in a deep dish. It was true, I had not dreamed it all up. But I had slept like a rock and admitted to myself that it is even more enjoyable now to have the entire mattress to myself in the morning, when I need to sleep.

Nikolai made his point again.

- You are on the way out into deep waters. I'm just telling you to be careful.

- But how could I say no to Liva? She just needs a little time to think about the situation with the fool, Mick. It is probably all over in less than a week.

- She will realize that Sabine is your girlfriend eventually.

- Maybe not. You were not there yourself, but the two girls get on very well. Sabine touched on something with a built-in sister-solidarity.

- Now you sound like a fool. On the other hand ... Have you considered that you're now two-thirds on the way with your project?

- What do you mean?

- Well, you were looking for a soul mate, a fresh, slightly wild-at-heart and an exotic type. Now you just need the exotic, don't you?

- Hahah. No, I have thrown that project away. I'm too fascinated and pleased with Sabine to continue my online dating. And Liva being a soul mate ended a long time ago.

- You just wait. The Good Samaritan will resurface in you and before you know it, you will be back comforting Liva sexually.

- No, stop it. All you always think about is sex!

I did not admit that during my day at the office, I had been considering the very same idea. Liva is still a very attractive woman and I have many wonderful memories of our time together, intimately as well. I found it a bit discomforting that Nikolai brought it up because I had tried to push the idea away earlier.

- Admit it. I can see you have thought about this yourself.

- Oh well, for a moment maybe. But it is not an issue.

But the seed was planted, and now watered as well. For the rest of the evening with Nikolai, I was a bit absent-minded but it was not just because of Sabine and Liva, who fought for attention in my subconscious. It became increasingly difficult to familiarize myself with Nikolai's own hardships. It seems they've found a new daycare, but apparently there is a run-in period, where one parent must be present during the first many days. They then phase out gradually, so the children can accustom themselves to be amongst other kids and staff. As far as I remember from my own childhood, parents just left. Not that I remember too much, but I still believe that children can sustain more than you think. The more fuss and disinfectant, the easier a child becomes dependent and infected. But to criticize other people's upbringing and care of their offspring is dangerous. It is obviously more allowed to comment on my choices and sometimes unplanned fate. At least I was not frightened by his exhortations. Of course I was in deep waters, but everything with Liva seems to be over in the near future. Surely she cannot expect to stay for a long time?

After an all too common café burger at the King Carrot and a few extra beers for dessert Nikolai and I parted. He returned to his wife and baby, I returned to ... Well, what should I call it?

When I let myself in, it was almost like watching a couple of friends sitting in the sofa on a cozy Friday evening enjoying a movie on the television. Pleasant enough, admittedly, but it felt a little strange to be a visitor at my own place. I got a glass of their wine, but was already drowsy after all the beers with Nikolai. I couldn't really follow the movie, so I decided to let them be film geeks and pull back.

I don't think there will be trouble falling asleep tonight. My entire world is revolving, and I am convinced that it's not only caused by alcohol. I'm really glad Sabine entered my life, but Liva needs support. Maybe it's best if I lay the cards on the table during the weekend? But what if that makes Sabine look bad? I'm going to turn off my lights and hope to fall into a deep sleep.

Monday 11th October, 2010

More Surprise

Ulrich called late this afternoon and invited himself to dinner. I didn't know whether Sabine would be at the university until late but I remembered that Liva would be going out to dinner with a friend. So this could be a very nice occasion to tell Ulrich about all the news over some good food at home with me. He would only be staying slightly less than two hours because this was his week to drive the youngest kid to some gym practice around here. But that suited me fine, and we agreed that he would show up around 7PM.

As Sabine had not come home by half past five, I gathered that she probably had an appointment with some fellow students and I was quite pleased to gently introduce Ulrich to my new life. However, he was very quick to notice some revealing details already when he passed through the living room.

- Why do you suddenly have so many plants? You always used to complain that they dry out before you get to water them.

- Well. It is linked to some things I have not had time to tell you about the last two times I saw you.

- Haha. Let me guess: You have a new career and started as a gardener?

- No, not at all. But I'm not exactly alone anymore. I have met a very sweet girl who moved in a week ago. And on

Thursday Liva came by and asked if she could stay here for a short time.

There. It was impossible to do any shorter, but I did expect to elaborate a bit.

- Liva? She got as a child with some new boyfriend. And where have you met a new girlfriend so suddenly?

I took a deep breath and told him about the whole project of searching for three women to enrich my life. About the first failed dates and how it also surprised me with Sabine. Ulrich and I are similar in several areas, partly because we tend to be thoughtful. I tried to explain that my very spontaneous decision with Sabine came about after a talk with Liva which reminded me of the joy of being two in everyday life. It was not easy to explain the logic, and Ulrich was almost as dizzy as myself.

- Do you seriously believe that Liva doesn't know that you and Sabine are lovers?

- Yes, so far we keep it a secret. I had planned to tell Liva about it during the weekend, but the occasion never really arrived.

All three of us, or rather four, including Xenia, had spent both Saturday and Sunday out walking, visiting parks and playgrounds. It had been one of the coziest little vacations I have ever experienced. Sabine and I had built up an intense desire over the two days, helped by our mysterious secret to Liva, so we could hardly wait to say goodnight and act tired after all the fresh air. There was something exciting about hiding it a bit longer.

- You know what? I think that Liva has found out about you. She's not lost behind a wagon, but is probably just showing respect and pretending nothing is going on.

- No, I don't think so. They've become good friends very quickly. And I must confess that I enjoy both the company and excitement.

When Ulrich had left and I cleaned up the kitchen, I thought a little more about his theory. Could he be right after all? I had not been present when Liva first met Sabine, and they had talked for several hours. Was it unlikely that I had a young and sexy girl living without having done something about it?

The door opened and Liva came into the kitchen with a sleeping Xenia in her arms. I signaled whether she wanted a glass of wine and she nodded on her way to tug in her daughter. When she came back after a few minutes, we sat at the table.

- She really is pretty cute, that girl Sabine. I understand that you fell for her.

- Ehm ... What has she told you?

- Honestly. How naive can you be? But we have had a lot of fun at your expense, old fool.

It turned out that Sabine and Liva had reached an agreement about both having a bit of fun, and they had succeeded in full. Women's wit comes in many shapes, but this was new to me. As I got over the initial embarrassment, I could not help but give Liva a giant hug. I was so grateful that she accepted my love for Sabine that it almost brought tears to my eyes. This could also explain their quick and good friendship - an open and honest agreement to deceive me, as long as it lasted. Of course Sabine had laughed so heartily when Liva went out for pizza that first night. Everything had already been planned there and then.

When Sabine came home, she could see that there was no longer a secret and she sat on my lap. My happiness made my insides melt. Here were the two most important women in my life and I could eat my cake and have it, too.

- You guys are really too much. Had I not loved you both so much, you would be kicked out the door right away.

- And then you could sit there with a story, you neither have children nor grandchildren to tell. Because you are not keeping Xenia.

We all laughed again, and I had to admit they had fooled me. With equal parts love and female ingenuity. Whether it was originally Sabine or Liva, who came up with the idea, is still uncertain to me, but I look forward to not having to fear hurting Liva's feelings in the future. Not least, I welcome that Sabine can now legitimately sleep in my bedroom. It was fun with the clandestine meetings, and it was nice to have my entire mattress to myself in the morning, but in the long run, I had probably ended up as a nervous wreck if the secret had continued.

Tuesday 12th October, 2010

Something to Celebrate

Dear Marie,

I promised to keep you informed of my project, and there has been a lot going on lately, so get yourself a huge cup of coffee before you read on.

Last time you heard about some rather unsuccessful dates and the young girl, Sabine. Thanks to her, I have been spared further dates. She moved in with me last weekend and I am exceedingly crazy about her. Therefore I see no reason to continue the project as such. Yes, make fun of me, but with this decision, I follow both my heart and my brain. If I had not fallen in love with Sabine, and she lived by herself, my attitude might be different. But she lived in a small, rented room nearby, and I thought that she could just as well have a room here. In addition, we fit together so well that she completely displaces my desire for a soul mate and the exotic. I already have anough emotional security and excitement, too.

Speaking of emotional security ... You remember Liva? It was after a talk with her, it dawned on me what I have been missing about being a couple. She needed to discuss her own situation, which has not been good recently. All the memories of our time together made me realize I wanted to spend more time with Sabine than just once or twice a week.

To complicate matters, Liva turned up here last week and asked if she could stay with me for a while with her daughter Xenia. She needs to think about her relationship with the father, Mick. Accidentally she arrived while I was at the office, but Sabine was home. Complicated? Yes, but continue reading.

The two of them decided to do a practical joke on me that I will never forget. It must be said that Liva did not know about Sabine. So she, I mean Sabine, pretended that she was just renting a room here. She and Liva became good friends quickly, but on some days I was pretty confused about having to keep my relationship with Sabine a secret in my own home. It wasn't until yesterday they confessed, and I do not really understand their motivations. It tuned out that Liva had known all along that Sabine and I are a couple. It could well be that I wouldn't have offered Liva to move in – for her own sake – if it were officially known to her that I had a new girlfriend living here. In any case I do not expect that Liva stays for long, but so far things are working fine.

We plan to have a party on Friday, right before to the autumn break, so if you want to come visit the capital, you are very welcome.

Sincerely,

Christian

It was also the girls' idea to have a party. After the combined discovery and confession yesterday, they thought that we should celebrate. I agreed to their idea, partly because I want to show my friends the new pleasures in my life, and partly because I will be leaving on a week-long trip on Saturday. The trip to Gran Canaria has been planned for months, and Sabine needs to work hard at a project paper all of next week anyway. This way I don't need to worry about the cleanup after all the guests. And I won't have to prepare a buffet, or whatever we decide to serve, all by myself.

We had fun talking about whether to choose a theme for the party and thought about 'Unconventional Housewarming,' 'Visit a different kind of homeĒ and others along those lines. But in the end we decided to just host an autumn party. It's fun to see people's reaction if they do not know in advance what they are getting into. And among my friends, Marie is currently the only one who knows about the entire, underlying story.

Come join our party at Carl Johans Gade.
This coming Friday you are invited to a festive evening in my penthouse. It is far too long since I last invited, and now it's time. I apologize for the short deadline, but sometimes stuff happens unexpectedly. Why not be a little impulsive?
There will be plenty of food and drink, but of course everyone is welcome to contribute with a bottle or similar of your own choice. Hope to get a confirmation from you by tomorrow. And there is also room for friends of friends.
Best regards,
Christian

Liva and Sabine invited their own friends individually via text messages, emails and phone calls.

The main reason why I have rarely hosted large parties, is my abhorrence to clean up for several days. Keeping my home neat and clean is a pleasure, but there are limits. Now I can leave with a clear conscience because Sabine and Liva have promised that they'll get everything back in shape. They even have a whole week to it.

Whether we get ten or fifty guests is impossible to predict. Liva has a mixed set of friends, but nobody really close. I doubt whether Sabine invites many from the university, but her best friend Judy from Argentina is arriving on Thursday. If I were to visit Denmark and Europe from South America, I would probably choose to travel in the summer, but if you've never seen the beautiful colors of our scenery in this season, it can probably seem exotic.

I expect to see Robert, Ulrich, Nikolai and William, and of course the trio Daniel, Kasper and Mikkel. I also hope that Laura will come by and maybe bring along some female friends. Benjamin doesn't like large gatherings, and I am also uncertain whether Marie bothers with the long journey, but now at least she has been given a full update. I am equally unsure about Elizabeth.

I will spend tomorrow at home and prepare a shopping list. Sabine has a couple of lectures followed by a meeting in her study group, so I expect to have my penthouse to myself during the day. Knowing that there is excellent company to come home to after a day at the office, however, is wonderful. Every other minute I keep thinking happily about how things have oddly happened. When I think back one month, I would never have imagined my life could be changed so radically and so quickly. It has almost escalated, and the peak so far was definitely the big and positive surprise last night. I am still a little duped, but it has led to some interesting experiences. Not least, a self-awareness about my own, perhaps misguided reasons. I am more and more convinced that I would have reacted differently if Liva had visited while I was there and Sabine was at the univeristy. How should I have explained that I no longer lived by myself? It would never occur to me to fabricate a white lie and hope that it succeeded.

Just before I was about to shut down my computer, a chat ticked in from Laura, thanking me for the invitation. I asked if she would be bringing any female friends and she expects them to be four in total. I didn't mention the specific reason for my party, so it will be interesting to get her reaction to my new life.

I hope to hear from the other guys tonight or tomorrow.

Wednesday 13th October, 2010

The Joy of Repetition

Liva and I were catching our breaths again after she had surprised me by sneaking into my bed in the middle of the morning.

- How come you are not at work?

- It's kind of quiet out there, so I could not help but live out some fantasies that I have had in the recent days. And I don't need to pick up Xenia until this afternoon.

- And you knew that I'd be home and Sabine is attending lectures?

- Yes. You can't begin to imagine how stimulating it has been knowing the two of you made love, though you have been doing so quietly ...

- I can imagine now. You certainly built up a good appetite.

We knew each others' bodies and preferences so well after the many years together and it had not seemed wrong at all to indulge. But I was a little surprised that Liva was so frank. Her personality has changed quite a lot the past couple of years. Not that I complain, when the result is to my advantage.

- Please don't think that I have entered a new, covert agreement with Sabine. But I have absolutely no scruples, and you appear resolved, too. Do you feel that you have been cheating on her now?

- Yes and no. The two of you have become close friends very quickly, but she knows that we have been together before. Technically, what we have done is wrong, but I have no regrets. We've just done something that we have done so many times before.

- Good, that's the way I feel about it as well.

We agreed that there was no reason to tell Sabine about this little digression, for it could very easily be a one time show. For old times sake, so to speak. For all I know, Liva will be moving out again during the next month. But if she stays, I will not refuse a repeat encounter when the opportunity arises. Anything is new and wonderful with Sabine, but there is also something irresistible about Liva, especially her newfound happiness, whether or not that is due to the absence of Mick.

She decided to pick up Xenia earlier than her regular schedule and I started on a somewhat late run compared to my normal routine. There was not much left of normal anymore, but I felt revitalized. My conscience was almost clean, but during the trip around the lakes I still felt a stab of anguish toward Sabine. It would be terrible if she gets hurt when there is no reason for it. On the other hand, she had originally replied to my profile knowing that I at that time was looking for three women. She may have thought that her winning personality and other qualities led me away from the idea of three. At the same time, she greatly contributed to Liva now sharing the home with us. No matter how I look at it, I cannot read her thoughts. Fortunately I do not need to playact in the future because of the morning's events, because it has always been natural for

Liva and I to give each other a hug or a kiss, even the company of Sabine.

I decided to wash and iron the linens after my run. Despite the fact that Sabine and Liva now use the same brand of lotion and perfumes, it was an important form of mental hygiene along with the purely physical act of removing any unwelcome traces.

During the ironing my thoughts traveled further. Elizabeth was the catalyst for ensuring I now in principle have two women in my life. Three if you count Xenia, but that is clearly outside the current equation. The major difference between Elizabeth's and my realization of our projects is that she sees her men separately, except for the summertime get-together, where they were all present. Her demands to the three partners had also always been fundamentally different than mine. Elizabeth wanted an intellectual, a handyman and a lover. Being a man, my wishes were in other directions, and without actually giving it special attention, I've never been in doubt that there needed to be a sexual aspect to all my desired women. And I think I've played my cards openly, because I was looking for three women. They should know it is not the one and only I look for.

Eventually it would be easier to keep my cool and avoid any unpleasantness if I could keep my women more distinct. All would undoubtedly have tumbled around me if Sabine had unexpectedly come home early this morning. What if a lecture had been canceled. I don't even want to think about that. Sabine needs to be in my life now, and with Liva it was just a nice breeze from the past. But she is also the perfect soulmate. Phew! There is no room at all for the third, the exotic.

Expecting that my two women would both be home for dinner, I started to cook dinner for all three of us. A big bowl of salad and a dish with lasagne based on salmon and spinach. We may as well start making plans for the meals on Friday, and what better conditions for that than a good dinner?

Later

They came home at the same time and had apparently met each other down the street. After a full hour at a café, where their intake was obviously more wine than coffee, they were both in good spirits. Wonder what their conversations had been about. It can be anything from general woman-like stuff to new secrets behind my back. In an attempt to avoid further paranoia, I brought up the party. I could expect about 10 guests, and it seemed that Liva expected four to seven participants, some friends and also a couple of colleagues. Sabine had handpicked three from the university, and then she reminded us that Judy from Argentina would arrive tomorrow evening. She will get Sabine's room, and none of us expect other overnight guests. Not unexpectedly Marie wasn't joining us, and she would be the only one with a long way home, apart from Judy, who will be staying a few days.

We planned to prepare a buffet. It is much easier to administer than serving meals of three to four dishes, and it also creates a more relaxed atmosphere. There will be some who do not know each other beforehand so without fixed seats, people are free to mingle or gather in groups as they prefer. It'll be a good and exciting evening, and today has also scored high on precisely those areas. My feelings for both Sabine and Liva are now more intense than anything I have previously experienced. I'm slightly in love with an old girlfriend and completely blinded by a new one at the same time. Not too bad after all.

Thursday 14th October, 2010

Enter Exotica

Maybe there really is a god or another entity answering prayers and fulfilling wishes. But he has a perfidious sense of humor. When I came home from yet another uneventful day at the office, in the week leading up to the whole country going on a fall break, I found not only Liva and Sabine in my living room, but in addition a woman who is a result of the Creator's very best talent.

Sabine's friend, Judy from Argentina, is adorable, enchantingly beautiful and the epitome of exotic in my definition. Her eyes are so dark brown, almost black, it is hard to see where her pupils end and her iris begins. Her black hair is shiny as in the most outlandish advertisements from Schwarzkopf. Her skin has a healthy glow of the sun's caress throughout her life. There was no doubt that I was exposed to the most beautiful sight in my life when I came home and found her in the room with Sabine, Liva and Xenia. They were all four engaged in dressing Xenia's dolls in different costumes, and perplexed I offered to start cooking dinner in the kitchen.

While I chopped vegetables and desperately tried to distract myself from the sight of Judy, she came out to assist me with the cooking. She speaks six languages fluently and when she got to know Sabine, she had also picked up some Danish, so there was no excuse of lacking linguistic comprehension on my part to send her back to the living room.

- You have a nice home here. Can I help you out with anything?

- Ehhmm ... I haven't quite figured out what I want to serve. But it will be something with vegetables in the oven. Au gratin with cheese. So you could start grating a large portion of my Parmesan, which is right over there.

- Oh, it already smells delicious with the garlic and fresh vegetables. Isn't it difficult to find good ingredients here so late in the year?

Her pronunciation and grammar was impressive. But with six languages already under full control, it might be easier with the next, even Danish.

- Oh, you know ... We have good imports from southern Europe and there are so many roots one can use depending on the season.

I could beat myself over the head with the chopping board for my lame comments, but was completely enchanted by her beauty. It was by no means easier to grasp the situation with Sabine and Liva being in the living room.

- Roots? Do you eat roots?

- Well, not roots as such, but as you can see here: beetroot, parsnips, potatoes, celery and carrots. We commonly denote them as roots.

- Ah, I see what you mean. But you also have chicken there, don't you? So you are not a vegetarian?

- Honey, I love meat. I just prefer to focus on fresh and crispy goods when I'm in charge of the cooking.

What's wrong with me? Here I am in my own kitchen and am flirting big-time with a strange woman, who on top of everything is my girlfriend's best friend while that same girlfriend is sitting in my living room playing with my ex-wife – and her little daughter. Have I gone completely mad? Or is there some truth to the saying that your appetite increases by eating?

I clearly have an appetite for Judy. Only a blind eunuch can resist her divine and inviting sensuality. Her rhythmic treating of the hard parmesan gave some clear associations, and I tried to abstract from the presence of grater. If I came near her beautiful hands, it should preferably be without a sharp tool nearby. I could provide my own tool.

What's wrong with me? Do I have the third woman, Miss Exotic, in my life now?

Over dinner all four of us wrote down suggestions to meals, we could prepare for a feast buffet tomorrow. I mostly wanted various salads and maybe some warm pies while Liva suggested a bit of Asian cuisine such as the classic sticks and sushi. Sabine and Judy were even more extreme, perhaps because of their experiences from South America. They would prepare savory empanadas, chimichurris and berenjenas. The latter was new to me, but when they explained that it was a kind of cooled, baked aubergines with parsley, oregano, garlic and peppers, I was convinced, absolutely perfect for a buffet.

All in all, our lists would satisfy most taste buds, and we agreed that the overall effort would result in an excellent, international tasting experience.

I found myself in the heavens of high expectancy. Culinarily, I could look forward to an exquisite event tomorrow and my visual pleasure was already filled to the brim. Here I was in my kitchen surrounded by nothing less than the cream of the best from my wildest dreams.

It was also nice to realize my wildest dreams did not include anything with threesomes or for that matter foursomes with all the beautiful women at the same time. Each woman at her own time, one might say. I agree with Elizabeth on that matter. It is important to keep things separated. And tonight, fortunately, there's no discussion about who is sleeping where. Both Liva and Judy know that Sabine and I are lovers. The little flirting earlier with Judy can be attributed to her warm-blooded nature as well as my deep-rooted fascination with beautiful women.

Best of all, however, was the inner heat I felt by being in the company of such wonderful ambassadors for their gender. One thing is the instinctive attraction, but it is even more rewarding to discover is our shared unity. I have become a victim of my own wild imagination to be close to exactly the three types of women I searched for on my online profile. Surprised, and not just a little proud!

Friday 15th October, 2010

Party

Preparations for tonight's party took up most of the day. We all took the day off and started out shopping this morning. It was amusing to see how Judy studied all the produce she certainly does not see at home in Argentina. But she was also surprised to see how many fruits and vegetables, Denmark can offer mid-autumn.

On several occasions I was delighted with the envious glances that I noticed from both shop assistants as other male shoppers. It was a nice little harem, I could display today. Maybe most people thought that I was a gay friend to a bunch of girlfriends? No matter, because I know better yourself.

Sabine does not seem jealous when Judy flirts with me but she is probably accustomed to the different culture often found in warmer countries. It can be a little difficult for me to balance on the border between friendly flirting and insinuations. For example, when Judy began to arrange fruit in unambiguous sexual constellations and especially when she compared her shapely breasts with a selection of melons.

- What size do you like the best? She asked, looking at me.

- Are you talking about melons or breasts now?

- Well, both, I'm curious.

- OK then. To me, the shape and firmness counts. In both cases. The size is not as crucial, to be honest.

Both Sabine and Liva laughed out loudly at my attempt to keep the conversation serious. They could easily see that Judy's teasing had some effect on me. Sabine was quick to follow up on the attack.

- Oh come on, we all know that size does matter.

- Enough, stop it. In that case we need to get some other fruits, how about bananas?

The atmosphere was charged already at the shopping trip, and while we prepared everything in the kitchen in the early afternoon, I also noticed how frequently Judy just accidentally brushed me when she passed by. I tried to check whether Sabine noticed it, but apparently she had her back to us every time. In a way, I was a little offended on Sabine's behalf that her friend so blatantly played up to me, but it was hopeless to do anything. And I admit outright that I enjoyed her interest.

And it wasn't without effect for Sabine that Judy heated me up like that, because on several occasions I had to let the energy out through hot kisses and embraces with my new girlfriend. Perhaps I also wanted to send signals to Judy about our relationship. But it seemed as if she became even more forceful in her flirtation.

I can't say if it was a coincidence or a planned act, that Judy flashed past my room on her way to her bath covering nothing of her perfect body, but what a sight! When it's my turn to shower, I think it better be in very cold water.

Liva has found a babysitter for Xenia, and we have arranged the living room and kitchen so there is seating for everyone.

150

We discarded the idea of seating everybody at one long table, but rather let people get together in groups. Our guests comprise a mixed bunch, and the gender distribution seems to be appropriate. I do not know Laura's girlfriends, but the quality of the other women is far above average. It will be fun to see how my friends tackle the evening.

I can readily imagine how especially Robert will do anything to get in close contact with Judy. She may be a bit too much for most others, but there will be lots of eyes on her. It will also be fun to see how Daniel and Laura are going to handle being in a larger company together. They will hardly get together again but will they be able to maintain the polished facade, if one or the other finds a new lover at my party, which leads me to think about how I would feel if someone goes for Liva. I have no right to feel jealous, but nevertheless it would be hard to ignore some feelings.

The whole party could in the worst case cause numerous crises. And then I could find myself being responsible for the chaotic emotional life of my buddies in the many months ahead. I haven't thought this angle through very well, but it is too late to do anything about it now. Maybe it was just the unexposed Judy exposing a lot of thoughts?

It's going to be nice getting away from it all tomorrow. I'm being stressed out over every change that has come so suddenly into my otherwise tranquil life. A week of total relaxation and a stack of good books can probably get my blood pressure back to normal. And who knows, maybe I will come home to everyday life again with only Sabine in the apartment. There is a possibility that Liva finds out Mick still deserves to get a chance, and I suppose Judy will continue her trip around Europe.

One thing is certain. I expect to come home to a clean apartment, all three of them gave me their word. But I also know myself well enough to realize I will hold back on the liquor in the evening for at least two reasons. Firstly, it is quite unpleasant to fly with a bad hangover, and secondly, I can't help but fix at least some of the mess before I go to bed. With a little luck I can lure any late guests to continue at the Park Café or somewhere else where they can carry on partying or have a final round. They can complain and call me a bad host, but they must respect that I have my principles.

They begin arriving in about an hour, and now the bathroom is finally vacant, so it is time for me to get ready. It would not surprise me if it becomes an involuntary cold shower after the three girls have had their serial baths. I could have suggested that the four of us showered together, but Judy would probably have convinced the two others and made me even more nonplussed than earlier during the day. The idea is worth dwelling on ... Perhaps it doesn't matter if there is only cold water in the pipes.

Saturday 16th October, 2010

Vacation Time

In about one hour, I am headed for Kastrup Airport in order to spend next week in Gran Canaria, and then I will have to find out about my friends' nocturnal escapades when I get home.

Our efforts to satisfy all taste buds fortunately seemed beyond all expectations, and although several people did not know each other at the start, everybody mingled thoroughly. As I had predicted, Judy was a bit of a draw for the men's attention and she almost rendered Robert speechless. He also brought a friend, I have not seen before, but they both fell nicely into the company, although his friend was a little loud. Next time I have a party, I will consider again whether friends of friends should also be invited. But Laura's friends enjoyed the attention from all the guys who definitely eyed Judy, but kept away from coming on to her. I once read that really beautiful women may perceive beauty as a curse because it can be intimidating to many men. Perhaps there's some truth to that, because it was evident that only a man as Robert tried his luck. However, it was without success, as I found out later ...

To my surprise, it seemed that Daniel and Laura almost started out again, at least they were often very close, both in the sofa and on the dance floor. It can sometimes be so much easier to resume a relationship than to start a new one, but from experience I know that it can be foolish as well. It is better to move on.

Sabine was engaged in a conversation with William and Nikolai for a long time and I understood they all had divergent views on the development of our news media. Every time I went to and from their discussion, I was proud to hear how Sabine could argue her case to my old friends. She is a hardworking woman, and it was obvious that she enjoyed the intellectual challenge.

Liva seemed to enjoy an evening without Xenia, and she was respectfully asked out on the dance floor, both by those who knew her from before and some who were new acquaintances. I hope she had an evening as nice as mine, even though it takes quite a bit to top my experience.

I had sent the party on into the night by explaining that I had to stop due to my trip late Saturday morning. About an hour later I first had a minor shock and then almost a revelation.

There was a lot to clean up, and I started to collect glasses, bottles and dishes to fill the dishwasher. The food was packed away already, and the girls had promised to get the apartment back in good condition next week.

So I sat in the kitchen and relaxed a little to the evening's last sip of wine and the rhythmic sound of automatic dishwashing in the dark. The shock was that Judy had sneaked in and suddenly sat on the table right in front of me.

- Weren't you supposed to pack and get to bed before your trip tomorrow?

- I thought you were out with the others.

- I was, too, but they don't dance so well and with all the loud music it's hard for me to follow conversations. So I chose to go back here instead.

- That I know too well. Not so much that I miss good dancing partners, but to conduct a conversation in the middle of a lot of noise can be difficult even for an old Dane like me. Hehe.

I tried to play down the rather special situation. At least to me it was mildly special seen in the light of our crystal clear flirtation earlier in the day.

- You're not that old after all. I've been with much older men.

Now she drove forward in the same track. She began to unbutton her tight blouse and tilted her head lightly.

- Do you feel old?

- Right now I feel like I'm seventeen. You are incredibly beautiful, Judy.

- Can you see me here in the dark?

- Honey, I can see you with my eyes closed!

She caressed her breasts and sat down on the floor in front of me. It was impossible to resist her sensuality. I could not prevent her from undoing my belt buckle and slowly open my pants. After some time I pulled her up from the floor to strip off her panther patterned skirt, but she averted my hands and continued her efforts. Eventually, it was not only her sensuality, I found difficult to fight, and I pulled myself a little back in the chair to give her a warning about the most likely outcome if she persisted. Which she did with bravura.

- Hmmmpffff ...

Her facial expression was invaluable - large eyes and dilated cheeks. How she managed a smile at the same time is a mystery, but she went to the kitchen sink and turned on the cold tap, which I understood perfectly. It is different for a woman who uses mouth and hands – and I have always been happy to enjoy the juices of a woman in smoother flows than what they are exposed to.

- What did you imagine? I gave you enough signals of the effect there.

- Let's just say that I was seized by the situation. Will you offer me a glass of wine?

- Sure. Come here. But tell me one thing. Why wouldn't you let me get closer to yourself? You could have avoided that mouthful, but it is perhaps a special time of the month or what?

- What do you mean?

- Well, you would not let me take your skirt off. I thought that you might be having your period, otherwise I cannot understand the context.

She laughed and simulated with clear gestures what she had just done.

- Haha. You're thinking, why this and not the other? Yes, you're right. I would not want you to have to clean the floor of your fine kitchen.

How wonderful that we could laugh about it and toast in the single glass of wine. I held her close to me and inhaled her warm and enchanting fragrance. Here was my third woman, with no discussion. Judy is as exotic as they come. Her divinely beautiful face is literally the icing on the cake of the even more fantastic body. I could die tomorrow and be a happy man who does not need to experience more in life.

In particular, it dawned on me like a thunderbolt from a clear sky, I would not wish to experience that Sabine came back from town, while I sat with Judy in a rather intimate embrace that could not be explained.

- You're right. I both need to pack and to be rested for my trip tomorrow. It's probably best that I go get some swimming trunks and t-shirts in a suitcase.

- Sleep well and thanks for a good party. I hope the weather is nice down in the Canary Islands.

I slept like a rock and never found out when Sabine came home later. She was still unconscious when I was in the shower and packed my toiletries at the top of my suitcase. I watched her while she lay sleeping in the morning light. Now I had already cheated on her twice in a week and she had only been my girlfriend for some ten days. What is going on in my life? I kissed her and felt the warmth of her body. A heat spread inside me with the knowledge of how much I love her.

Why can I not resist the temptation to involve myself in wrong adventures with both my former wife and with Sabine's own good friend? I may never get to know the psychology of women, but the most bizarre thing is that my own actions can give so much food for thought!

Nevertheless, I have to say that my original plan of the project was a success. Carpe diem has become Carpe donna, and I cannot repress a certain degree of complacency, although it is mixed with astonishment.

Next stop Kastrup Airport and I have packed a good handful of books to distract me from all the women in my life. The next couple of days will be spent with crime novels and neither emails nor updates in my journal.

Monday 25th October, 2010

Homecoming

When I'm traveling, my dreaming is often more active than when I'm at home. Last week was no exception, there was so much for the subconscious to process from the past few weeks. To my chagrin the dreams didn't offer deep insights or solutions, but especially two dreams kept recurring.

In the first one I walked around in a building under construction. I could see that most of the walls were freshly painted, but in a few places they still had to install lights, because wires from the electrical outlets were sticking out here and there. It would also appear that the interior decorator experimented with different styles. At the entrance to one room I saw an oriental style sliding door with rice paper and a dark, fine wooden frame. It slid open easily and elegantly when I pulled it aside, but the space behind was empty - I was looking for something but did not know quite what. Further along the corridor I tried a more ordinary-looking door, and it was somewhat heavy to open. I could see that it was much more solid, probably a fire proof door. In there I also looked around in vain. At the next opening I noticed a saloon-door, and when I stretched my neck to look over it, it dawned on me that I was looking for a stairway or an elevator, but was trapped on this floor.

In my second recurring dream, I was climbing a ladder, placed on a solid surface, but it was not leaning against a wall. It was a fun challenge to gently move farther and farther up while I was holding it in a comfortable angle, so I wasn't falling forward or backward. But without having noticed how many steps I had reached, I suddenly panicked. I looked down and got dizzy.

Both dreams had me waking up bathed in sweat. It was quite warm in the hotel room, and it was pretty uncomfortable every time. On several nights I spent a half hour on my balcony to cool off. Why can't my dreams give me a few ideas for solutions? I was well aware of what the images told me, and did not need reminders.

Otherwise the days were spent on the planned relaxation, good books and good meals, so despite an unearthly early departure back Saturday morning, I was pleased to have had a much needed respite. When I entered my apartment, I immediately noticed that my entire hall was freshly painted. The furniture in the living room had been rearranged, but my bedroom was untouched. Apparently there was no one home and I looked forward to a long bath after the many hours flying back.

I had another surprise in the bathroom. Judy was in my Jacuzzi and appeared to doze. The jet streams were paused, so I could clearly see her body in the clear water. I stood there spellbound and enjoyed the sight as she opened her eyes. A broad smile appeared on her beautiful face.

- Welcome home. Did you have a nice holiday?

- Oh, you bet, but it's also nice to be home again. You are very beautiful!

- Come give me a little company. We'll be alone awhile, because Liva is attending something she calls the baby theater with a friend and Xenia. Sabine is at the university to finalize the assignment due on Monday.

This is what I would call "An Offer You Can't Refuse!"

At some point along the way I had an idea to fit some anti-slip coating on one edge of the tub, but we avoided injuries. Finally we got the opportunity to explore each others' wishes, and it was all carried out slowly and softly. I was happy that she had chosen to defer the further exploration of other European countries.

After a much needed afternoon nap alone in my bedroom, I got up and found all the girls in the living room. They had arranged the sofas so they could all hang out and watch television from good angles. Previously there had rarely been a need for more than two people to watch the screen simultaneously, but the new layout was both cozy and practical.

They all wanted to hear about my vacation and I showed them some rather uninteresting pictures by connecting my camera to the big flat screen. I had not been on any tours, but talked enthusiastically about a couple of excellent restaurants that had served perfect meals of both meat and fresh fish. That worked as cue words and we all headed to the kitchen in a strange mixture of collective, lovers and good friends.

- Thanks for shining the place up so nicely. I hate to repaint, and the entrance looks really good now.

Sabine laughed and said that Judy had been extremely active the last week. She had also repainted the room originally intended for Sabine and the one now occupied by Liva and Xenia. During the week Sabine had entrenched herself in my bedroom with her assignment and Liva had acted as the older sister to the others doing cooking and general care. I had come back to a home that was radically different on many fronts.

Because of my slightly late nap I was not tired, when the others began to yawn, but I was pleased nonetheless to be alone with Sabine. And we spent most of Sunday alone in my bedroom. Last night we all went for an early evening stroll and we ended up bringing home five different pizzas. I was amused to find out I was not alone in having difficulty choosing.

During the entire Monday here at the office, I have found myself in a strange high of joy and amazement at how my life has changed. It's like a completely different kind of dream, one of those I do not want to be woken from.

Tomorrow evening I have an appointment with Daniel, Kasper and Mikkel and I am looking forward to hearing more about their night after the party. They will hardly believe me when I tell them about the development at home. I don't want to jinx the whole thing by describing my paradise in each and every detail.
But if only they knew...

Tuesday 26th October, 2010

Evening Beers

Dear Christian,

I hope you had a good party last Friday. Thanks again for your invitation and your comprehensive update, it was an amusing read. Apologies for not getting back to you sooner, but I've been to Jutland for a while to wind down. It doesn't look too promising to sell the house here in Kalundborg, but maybe next spring?

It sounds like you have your hands full with women. It was an interesting point you made about Liva and Sabine – they both figured you'd have a problem with letting Liva move in if she knew that Sabine and you were lovers. If that's the case and they planned it together, they both have a very good insight into your personality, and their plan worked smoothly after all.

I am surprised at your choice to live with Sabine, having known her such a short time. Maybe you just had enough of being alone, and you certainly have done something about that.

Do keep me updated.

Sincerely,

Marie

It is a pity for Marie, she is stuck with an unsold house in Kalundborg. Her self-chosen exile may have worked in the short run, but I miss her humor and can read between the lines that she is not on top. She would have been a good observer at the party. I cannot figure out whether I should tell her about the further developments. She does not know that I now also have Judy here.

Dear Marie,

It is sad that you are stuck in Kalundborg with the house. Good to see you got away on holiday after all ... I was in Gran Canaria for one week and it was nice to get a little distance to everything. You are so right when saying that I suddenly have my hands full.

So far, I have chosen to focus on the positive, and there is plenty of that. Our daily lives work out well on all operational issues and I am extremely pleased to have a new spice in my life. Lower the price of your house and come back to Cph!

Sincerely,

Christian

What was it that made me not tell about Judy? Marie could hardly ruin anything by, for example, gossiping to Sabine. Or to Liva, for that matter. This was the core of my new dilemma. Liva knows that Sabine and I are a couple, and she has agreed to stay with us as a friend. That Liva and I had our single session does not mean that I love Sabine any less. But neither Sabine nor Liva is aware that Judy managed to seduce me. They are very knowledgeable about the effects, Judy has on me and they teased me with my boyish flirtation, but it's different now, when there has been hot and secret sex in the picture.

Judy also knows that Sabine and I are together. She knows that Liva and I have been married, but she does not know that Liva still manages to get me in the sack. Sabine knows nothing of my escapades with Liva or Judy, and that's how I prefer things to continue. That is if we continue to all live together in my apartment. I have to chat with Liva soon about her future with or without Xenia's father, Mick.

Later

I arrived a little after half past six to my appointment with Daniel, Kasper and Mikkel. As so often before Mikkel had not yet arrived.

- Hello, nice to see my delay is once more trumped by Mikkel.

- He is at a conference in London, so you can forget that trump, Kasper commented in his dry form.

- Well, at least I can go order a round of beers. Same as usual?

We each have our different favorite beer, and I got handed a standard order at the bar before I put my heart into a discussion about the benefits of syncing all calendars, email accounts and what do I know between mobiles and computers. I was more curious to hear about how their night at the Park Café had developed last Friday.

- Good to see you again, anyway. Did you continue at Park last Friday?

- To be quite honest, I cannot remember how I got home, Daniel said.

- Haha. Not the first time. But I hope you had a good evening?

- It was certainly some super delicious food, you served. And even if you threw us out, we continued a few hours first at the Park and later on Fedthas.

- But that hot chick, Judy, she left us quite early.

- Yes, she surprised me, too, at home in the kitchen, but she said she had trouble following conversations in the noisy surroundings.

- Oooh. Did you have a little nice time with her?

- No, we just talked over one last glass of wine. I had to get up early and leave for my vacation the next morning. But she is a fascinating woman, don't you think?

There was a general agreement among all three of us that Judy didn't need to work hard to catch any man. Had it not been because I'm now officially with Sabine, it would have been a great pleasure to brag about my little experience with Judy.

- Do you regret the fact that you are with Sabine?

- Not at all, and without her I would never have met Judy. But it can be a little frustrating when she flirts so intensely.

- And nothing happened when she surprised you in your kitchen?

- No, stop it already. Besides, she had her period.

They both looked at me with huge eyes. Oops, I had almost revealed it.

- Well, it came up during the conversation. We just sat and talked a little before I packed my bags. That's all there was to it.

During the rest of our after-hours beers I didn't bring up the subject of Judy again, even I could hear it all sounded a little woolly. But Daniel and Kasper didn't press on, quite to the contrary, they commented on Sabine being such a nice, fresh girl. They mentioned how I should hold on to her, fortunately without implying she had behaved challenging. My mind was in a complete chaos when I left the boys and slowly walked home through the city.

I could not let go of the idea about how sad I would be if I found out Sabine had been with another last Friday. This is in no way connected with the fact that I on the same evening and without too many scruples had a very intimate thing with Judy. But I know myself and it does not affect my feelings for Sabine. She could just as well – being so young, fresh and inviting – fall for a temptation on the way? The difference is that I cannot be sure whether a temptation for her would evolve into a threat to our relationship. It is different with my little adventure, because Judy is leaving soon anyway.

Deep down, I am aware that I am trying to cling to a justification that does not quite work. The fresh air on the walk home has not helped clearing my tumultuous mind, and it is quite OK that Sabine has already fallen asleep. I need to sleep and don't need weird dreams.

Wednesday 27th October, 2010

Happiness

This morning I got up early and prepared breakfast for
Sabine before she was off to her lectures. If she took it as an
act marked a bit by my conscience is impossible to say, but
she looked very happy when she entered the kitchen after
showering.

- What excellent service! I thought you still were sleeping.

- Sometimes I can wake up early, even if you do not wake
me with kisses and caresses. Anyway, I need to proceed with
some business from home today, so it's good to get started a
little early.

- Are you skipping your morning run?

- No, but change is good. I'd rather pamper you now and
then I can take a break from work at midday and run before
lunch.

When we had finished our coffee and toast, Liva and Xenia
joined us, and I prepared more coffee. Judy tended to sleep
in, but she had no obligations like the rest of us. There was
no reason to repaint the living room or anywhere else, and
her efforts as thanks for the shelter was already far beyond
what one might expect. In all respects.

- Judy asked me yesterday which sights we could
recommend a tourist, and I could not really think of
anything better than Kronborg. What do you think? Liva
asked as she packed lunch for Xenia.

- Kronborg Castle is surely a classic, although it is way up north, I replied.

Apparently Sabine has never really been interested in our local attractions and had no better proposal. I understod that Judy intended to stay in the country for some time yet and silently welcomed the news. Simultaneously a minor conflict arose between emotion and reason once again, but I had better get used to that.

During the morning I wrote a good pitch for a new customer and rewarded myself with a long run. In order to not be disturbed by a lot of thoughts along the way, I had loud music in my ears and kept a somewhat faster pace, so it was only my breathing and rhythm, I focused on. Sometimes the brain needs to relax completely, and I am lucky enough to know the best ways to do so. After a long shower, I was in my bedroom putting on lotion when Liva knocked gently on the door frame.

- Do you have a moment?

- Yes, of course. Just let me get dressed.

- I don't think you need to. I had a da capo from the other day in mind.

The 'moment' she had referred to became almost an hour but we were both aware that we had this opportunity for ourselves, so there was no hurry. Meanwhile, I forgot all about wanting to talk to her about Mick, about her prolonged stay here and everything else in the world. It was fabulous to experience how we could return to the shared enjoyment. The joy of repetition can be quite amazing. Without comparison at all, this might also be the reason that I can enjoy a few select movies over and over again and each time get a new experience out of it.

But afterwards I needed to talk to her about Mick.

- Say, I haven't heard whether you have contacted Mick after the holidays?

- He called me yesterday because he could not figure out how to turn on the washing machine.

- Is that a bad joke? Didn't he wonder where you were?

- It's just so typical. It's become a power struggle, I think. It must indeed be clear to him that I have not been there for a long while, and he got back on Monday. I'll never get him to show interest, let alone now. Can I stay here a little longer?

I pulled her close and felt a stab of pity. My previous expectations that she would already be gone when I came back from vacation made me quite ashamed.

- Of course you can, honey. Just as long as you need.

Emotions won again, but a part of my reasoning could also hoist the flag. As long as Liva lived here too, it would be more difficult for me to fall for the temptation of Judy because I was less likely to practically find times when only Judy and I would be home alone.

- Aren't you home quite early, by the way, I thought you picked up at Xenia around five?

- They called from the nursery school and said she was ill. She lies asleep inside our room and then I heard that you were showering.

- I am really sorry about everything with Mick. But I don't know what I can do.

- You already helped plenty. Thanks for letting us stay here. Let's go to the kitchen and prepare a traditional Danish dinner. I bought some juicy slices of pork on the bone on my way home

- Hehe. A real Holger Danske meal. Very appropriate for Judy after Kronborg.

We agreed to cook in the oven to avoid too much frying smog, but when Judy and shortly after Sabine came home, there was an unmistakable smell of Danish cuisine throughout the apartment. Judy initially thought that it was a little grotesque to eat that portion of a pig, but was convinced after the first taste. Sabine teased her and mentioned a line of South American specialties, which were at least as noteworthy.

I had also found some snaps to comply with tradition, and we all crashed in sofas a few hours later. Well fed and happy, maybe a little intoxicated.

It's been a good day. All three women are now half asleep in front of an unexciting movie on television. They're so lovely, and it's annoying to me that I cannot get to share this joy with my friends.

Oh, but of course!

Dear Elizabeth,

Thanks to your challenge and provocation to find three women, I am now the happiest man in the world. Inside my living room is a representative, each the best of its kind I think, for all my three favorite women. It is not entirely without problems, but certainly with more gains than I had imagined. You see, unlike you, we all live together. It sometimes causes a little difficulty with the logistics, as you can probably imagine.

In close confidence, I can tell you that Sabine doesn't know that I also had a couple of intimate hours with both Liva and Judy. You were not at the party, but if and when you ever meet Judy, you will certainly understand. And you have heard about Liva, so it will hardly surprise you that we were tempted to relive some good times.

I expect that Judy travels on within a week or two, and until then I will do my best to keep everything working. Regarding Liva's future, I imagine that she at one point finds her own place again. But as I understand it, she is done with Xenia's father, Mick.

Sabine is as beautiful as ever, and I'm being very careful. So you do not need to warn me against the obvious dangers, I find myself in. I am well aware that it is risky, but who doesn't dare ... Hehe.

Sincerely,
Christian

It was not to triumph, but I felt so on top. And if there was anyone I could share my joy with, it was Elizabeth.

Thursday 28th October, 2010

Perspectives

Benjamin sent me a text message this morning regarding a new brunch restaurant he had read about, and as we both had a quiet day, we met a couple of hours later for a very late breakfast. Some would even call it a late lunch, but these days one can find places where they serve this delicious meal way until the early afternoon hours.

We both support the motto that one should eat breakfast like a king, lunch like a prince and dinner like a poor man. However, we rarely live by the rule and our brunch today covered the calorie basis of least two regular meals.

As he stirred the syrup served with the pancakes, I noticed he seemed a little distant and he must have thought of yet another political issue. He often investigates some strange topics and can talk about details for several hours, once he gets started.

- Do you remember the oil rig that caught fire and sank earlier this year?

- Oh yes. BP got a serious problem there. But people forget quickly, unfortunately. Have you found new data on that?

- You better believe it. I was curious because there was so much in the media about how large a quantity of oil actually leaked out although official reports varied greatly and it is probably hard to say with certainty.

- But you have become wiser, I can imagine?

- As far as I have read, it was about the amount of the Exxon Valdez every four days for an extended period of time. It is really saddening, I think.

- That sounds incredible. Wasn't Valdez the biggest oil disaster before the platform?

- No, not even the biggest, and think about it: Every fourth day as much oil escaped from underground, as what leaked in total from that huge ship.

How could I bring up my small everyday problems, when there were issues with totally different perspectives? When I had previously tried to point our conversation toward women, he had not shown great interest.

- Well. It undeniably puts everything else in a whole new light. Here we are fighting with our indifferent challenges while the world quietly is about to go under. By the way, what is that beeping all the time? Are you getting a lot of text messages?

- Haha. No, it's just my new phone telling me that I have a brunch appointment with you. I cannot figure out how to delete the reminder, but it will pass after some time.

He fished out his mobile and tried to make it behave. He failed, so I reached out and fixed it for him, but he continued his svada on Valdez and Deepwater Horizon.

- According to Wikipedia, Valdez was not particularly severe compared to other registered accidents. It is far down the list. I've never heard about many of the others.

- That's how it is with the media. If you miss a headline one day, the news will be replaced by something else within less than a week.

Similarly, I have recently been intrigued by the local news in my life. Just within the past month I have had several huge headlines rapidly replacing each other on the billboard of my consciousness. At least my talk with Benjamin provides food for thought, and perhaps it is a good idea to perform an intellectual summary again tomorrow.

Despite the solid brunch I accepted a dinner invitation from William, who was home by himself and wanted some company. His wife and kids were at the theater, and like he said we both needed some food. It suited me perfectly fine to get a little break from my apartment now fully occupied by women, and William is a true master in a kitchen.

When I arrived, I inhaled the wonderful scent of spices and steamed fish.

- Oh, you've outdone yourself. And I've eaten a massive brunch earlier today. But now my appetite returns.

- Well, you know the saying that the more you eat, the bigger your appetite?

- Haha. Certainly, and that can be true for more than food.

I tried, maybe a little inelegant, to bring up the appetite for women. But he didn't catch my point.

- Are you becoming an alcoholic?

- I was thinking about the more you have sex, the more pleasure you can get.

- Sex is a little exaggerated. There is so much in the media about it that I completely lose the urge sometimes.

It was impossible to explain to a man, who had followed the traditional path of a regular family, how I'd found myself in a new spring in the middle of the late summer of my life. We are both turning fifty shortly, and we have had completely different lives. Our interest in good food is the same, and we communicate well. But I could not share the joys or the potential problems, my choices resulted in. In a way, it was nice to just spend an evening where I for a moment could relax in the good company of a friend.

The best thing was that I felt the inner happiness and awareness that I have achieved a fantastic goal of having three of the world's best women in my life.

Friday 29th October, 2010

High Stakes

Dear Christian,

How nice to hear that you have found happiness with your version of the model. Three women under one roof and then on top of that exactly the types you set yourself to find! It is incredible how we can have our wishes fulfilled when daring to go a little outside the traditional framework. I do not think it would have worked to me. It could easily have generated an element of competition between the men, but it is not the biggest difference in our respective ways to organize ourselves. As I understand it, your three women are not all aware of their roles. Especially with Sabine you play high stakes, and I have to warn you, despite your assurances. One thing is to not be able to choose and a second is to have a free choice on all shelves.

Beware of Nemesis.

In the meantime, I am sure you enjoy every moment, so best of luck!

Love

Elizabeth

She is right. It is a dangerous game, but I cannot in any way explain to Sabine how her two good friends have their claws in me. The only thing planned on my part was that she moved from her rented room and in with me. Everything else has just happened more or less randomly, I think. We only managed to get a few days where it was just the two of us, and then Liva popped in unannounced. I have wondered about their little joke, where Sabine pretended she was just a lodger. There is no doubt that I would have been skeptical about letting Liva move in, if I had to admit to her that I had a new, young girlfriend living with me. And if they could think up that little drama, could they also both be aware that Liva and I have been together again? According to Liva, there is no reason to cause Sabine alarm and I don't feel there's anything different with Sabine. When Judy came into the picture, already the first few days were laden with sexual innuendo, but that could be explained by her extreme personality. I've been incredibly fortunate throughout, but there is no guarantee that it can continue.

What if Liva decides to stay put here? Imagine if we could achieve a harmonious balance, where we find our places in each others' lives. And if Judy were to end up hanging around, too, just for the sake of thinking it over ... They have fun together and I am sure that Judy would not complain about the situation. As for Liva, she is well aware that I am officially with Sabine. The big question is whether I can keep myself from Liva and Judy over a longer period of time. As things are now, I feel it can be done with an extra dose of willpower. They are all beautiful, but it should be possible to limit the sex to Sabine. In that case I will gain a much better conscience and a little flirtation with Liva and Judy does not hurt.

It is rather unfortunate that I have such a hard time talking to my friends about all of this. Fortunately, Elizabeth gives good feedback in emails, but it would have been nice with little input from another guy or two. Bringing all the details up has an unpleasant effect – it seems partly as a luxury problem, and partly as bragging. It's not entirely unlikely that I have painted myself into in the corner of all corners.

If there is one guy I could perhaps tell everything, it would be Robert. He has recovered from his recent breakup, and is probably even active with a lot of women, so there will be no competition about who gets the most right now.

Hi Robert,

How are you doing with your online dating profile? Can you cope with it? I had a nice, relaxing vacation in the week after the big party and got a pleasant surprise when I got home: Judy had not left but spent the week repainting a few rooms in my apartment. She still lives here and so does Liva. And yes: I'm still in love with Sabine, so my life is now surrounded by three wonderful women. It all seems quite surreal, and I could use a man talk in not too long.

Let us find an evening next week if you can find the time among your many dates.

Have a nice weekend

Christian

I'd better be getting home from the office. Our unwritten rule is that if one is not present at half past six, there's likely to be an appointment with others and no attending dinner. But the alternative is to walk alone into some bar and hang out among the city's other frustrated guys until the problems are diluted. I would much rather return to my women.

Maybe I will find an occasion during the weekend to unveil my little digression for Sabine. Either that or make a firm decision that it will not happen again. The latter is probably the easiest, though the temptations still seem insurmountable. If I start out making it absolutely clear to Sabine how much I love her, it may be easier for her to accept? And she knows both Judy and Liva well enough to know I would not run off with any of them – so she should not feel uncomfortable or threatened.

But it is a breach of faith on my part no matter how I look at it. I could not have told her the truth earlier. Every time I saw the individual stories as isolated events with a woman who would soon be gone, and which in no way diminished my feelings of Sabine. She has always been highly valued and still is.

Elizabeth's warning of Nemesis is hovering over me like a great, black cloud in partnership with my nagging conscience. It is so unfair, because although I confess to being partly to blame for this situation, I've also been a victim of circumstances entirely beyond my control. If Liva had been in a happy relationship with Mick, she would never have moved in. If Judy had not come to visit Sabine, I would have been happy without an exotic dream-girl in my life.

On the way home I'll visit a Blockbuster outlet and find a good handful of movies. It will divert my thoughts, and I hope they are all three at home tonight. Spending a peaceful evening in their company is good for my soul, a bit like when I was a kid and found out how nice it was having a lot of girls around me. Back then life was somewhat easier because the sex was, at most, some poorly defined fantasy. I hardly dared kiss even the sweetest, and now it is possible to both hug and kiss all the three wonders, I'm surrounded by.

I'm the luckiest man in the world!

November

Monday 1st November, 2010

A Place for Experiences

Sabine had a good idea Saturday morning. Her lack of interest in our national tourist attractions that could be something to show Judy, was counteracted by a girly shopping trip across the sound to Malmoe. None of them had visited Sweden before and I told them that there were many good shops over there and reasonable prices. But I also refused to join them because all I would have bought for myself – a few beers – would be considerably more expensive. And the prospect of visiting one clothing store after another, even with such delightful company, I could do without.

Instead I decided to go for an extra long run, while the washing machine took care of of the growing amount of laundry my extended household entails at the moment. Not only was there more long hair in the bathroom as a result of living with three adult females. The sheer number of used towels, kitchen towels and dish cloths appeared to have exploded.

My run left me thoroughly cold, because I had not kept an especially high pace, but instead jogged along twice the distance I normally do. It was an exquisite luxury to relax in the warm Jacuzzi when I returned exhausted to a comfortably quiet apartment. Liva was probably out walking with Xenia, perhaps at a playground close by if I had to make an educated guess. I put on a CD with Buddha-Bar and let myself float to the music and water massage.

I must have almost fallen asleep, because it startled me when Liva gently slipped down beside me. She smiled devilishly and got comfortable.

- I suppose you don't mind a little company?

- You bandit, you. You know very well that I cannot say no to you.

- Hehe, luckily it's just your willpower that's lacking strength.

I don't understand how she is able to keep such great a figure even after giving birth and without much effort at exercising. She has always contributed it to good, healthy genes, and there must be something correct about that theory. She also has a lavish consumption of various lotions that are either tightening or promise other slimming results. I do not believe that they work, but the result is indisputable, and I could not hide my enthusiasm for her.

Again it struck me that it could be a good idea with a non-slip coating on one edge of the porcelain, but we survived without incident. I thought that this could easily be the last time because I also remembered my plan to stay away from temptation and focus on Sabine. One last time can't hurt, and it was great to give in to the beautiful body I probably know almost as well as my own. It's always exciting getting to know a new woman, but there is also a great charm in being so familiar in the physical area that there are small stories associated with practically every single, well placed caress.

After Sabine and Judy came home loaded with shopping bags, we all sat down with drinks in the living room and invented a new game. They began by doing a catwalk, at first with their new acquisitions, and later with a wide selection of all the wardrobes in the house. We were then to guess which films they parodied. Not that the dresses helped much, but as I recall, it included Pretty Woman, When Harry Met Sally and There's Something About Mary. No, it was clearly not their disguises revealing which films we had to guess. But the entertainment was world-class and I looked forward to strip Sabine from the last costume when that time came.

Unlike last Sunday where Sabine and I spent most of the day in bed, we were all very cultural yesterday. It was Liva's proposal that we should go visit the Glyptotek, and when we had explained to Judy that the place is a museum of ancient and modern art, she was almost irritated that we had not told her about it before. And there was even free admission on Sundays, which suited her well after the costly excursion the day before. I teased her that she should try to get a grip on her fiery temper, and she calmed down again. If you can call it calming down when she immediately bullied us to get ready for departure.

It turned out that we had different favorites among the many departments and we agreed to split up and meet in the café after an hour, where we could each respectively enjoy paintings, sculptures and the various collections. After half an hour, I went down to find the toilets and came across Judy, who was also on her way down to the basement. It took us just a few nanoseconds before we found the roomy toilet for the disabled, and locked us up inside. Suddenly there were other needs to be covered. And I repeated the admonition to myself that it really was the last time with Judy.

We arrived at the café just before Liva turned up with Xenia and we found a table just as Sabine came out of the souvenir shop. It seemed that I had succeeded once again to hover on the cloud of fortune.

When we walked out of there, I saw a poster with the Glyptotek slogan: "The Glyptotek is a place for experiences" it said. Yes, indeed, it has met that obligation today!

All day today I have alternated between the good memories from the weekend and my growing, dark conscience. Had I not promised myself to be faithful to Sabine and resist temptations from Liva and Judy? Why can't I trust myself? How can I avoid being so fascinated by all three of them? It is not that I disappoint Sabine, though I fell asleep very early last night. I could not keep myself awake for the last film we had from Blockbuster and I blamed it on my long run Saturday and the immense cultural experience from the Glyptotek. It was fun to see Judy's facial expression when I mentioned the cultural experience as being a cause to my fatigue.

Tonight I will in turn focus exclusively on Sabine. It better not become too obvious, but I will find a balance. I miss her and can definitely tell her how much I love her without acting. Sometimes it takes a little comparing before we find our preferences. It's only because I've been all around the Glyptotek, that I know where I would rather spend more time. Eventually I'll get what I want.

It is easy to justify to myself, but probably smartest to waive the lengthy explanations when I sit down to cleanse my conscience for Sabine. I just hope she listens and will receive with her beautiful, open mind.

Tuesday 2nd November, 2010

An Important Conversation

All my good intentions to have a thorough chat with Sabine fell apart last night. Not because I was lacking the energy, but she came home very late after a long day of intense studies with her study group.

I left the office early to be home before half past five. It's always exciting to see if dinner is for two, three or all four of us. Oh well, five if you count Xenia, but she still did not really eat adult food. I found only Liva and Xenia in the kitchen when I got home and we had the latter fed while we enjoyed a few glasses of wine. Liva said that Judy had found some salsa dancing somewhere in the city and we certainly could not expect her to come home early.

As the clock turned seven, we decided to cook ourselves some pasta. If Sabine managed to show up, she could join us or otherwise heat up the remains if she didn't come home until later. It was almost like in the old days fussing around in the kitchen and chopping garlic, tomatoes and herbs with Liva. Everything else aside, we could just as well have been a happily married couple. But everything else was certainly not aside. She was in a self-chosen exile from her new boyfriend, who was even the father of her child. At one time or another she needs to make a decision affecting both her own and Xenia's future. I was in a situation that I might have wanted, but absolutely could not foresee the consequences of. If I ever encounter the real spirit in a bottle, my first wish would be that I am entitled to an unlimited number of wishes.

- There is something I want to talk to you about. We know each other very well and confidentiality is a given, I said, but before I continued, she asked

- Have you been with Judy?

That Liva had imagined the possibility did not surprise me, but I was still a little shocked by the very direct question.

- What makes you think so?

- She is the prototype of your third favorite. Sabine has told me about your online dating profile, where she contacted you initially. I see myself as your soul mate, and she is perfect as the fresh type, isn't she?

She read me like an open book. But it's not really that strange, because we know virtually all corners of each other after the many good and bad years.

- It is true that Sabine is perfect and the one I want. Do you think she suspects I had a few adventures? Have you talked to her about it?

- No, she hasn't asked me or brought the subject up with me. And they're very close friends, so it could also be possible that Judy would not get serious about her otherwise pretty clear signals. But I know you. You could not resist, if you had the chance. Am I right?

- I cannot lie to you, you know that. But promise me that you will not tell Sabine about it. Each and every time I have thought that it would not change my feelings for Sabine, and it was the same when I was with you.

- Each and every time? So, you've had something going with Judy for a while?

- I haven't been counting, but please understand. It's no different than with you and me. We have something that is no threat to Sabine. But I still feel guilty.

- I am certainly glad that I hit the spot. It was precisely this, you needed to talk about wasn't it?

- It was my guilt, of course. Not necessarily as specific, but I would so hate to hurt Sabine. She's worth fighting for, and I just have to find the right solution.

Liva advised me to have a talk with Sabine. As I had figured by myself, I should not bring up the temptations of Judy, but focus on how much I love Sabine. Frankly, I think Liva wanted the best for me, and I devoured her good advice. After dinner and the good talk, I went into my bedroom to think things over. It was irritating that Sabine took so long to get home. Now I had really built up courage and good phrases that could release me from the bad feelings which struggled in my consciousness. While I was waiting for her to come home, I also realized that it might all just be something I fought with inside myself. She had not shown signs that anything was wrong. And as Liva had correctly made me aware of, Sabine and Judy are very close friends. So it is probably also a matter of trust between the two of them, isn't it?

I woke up when Sabine lay down to sleep in my bed. She must have gotten home substantially later than usual. I kissed her and could feel that she was more inclined to fall asleep in my arms than to end a hectic day with physical activity.

- I love you, Sabine.

- Mmm. Thank you. I love you too. Sleep tight.

Have I been worried without reason? I was suddenly wide awake, and lay there with my mind racing. When I could hear by her breathing that she had fallen into a deep sleep, I walked into the living room and poured myself a brandy. I must have been sitting there some time and just looked out the window while I tried to get a grip on my life.

Luckily I was not disturbed or tempted by either Judy or Liva. It was very quiet in my otherwise recently more lively apartment. It's at hours like these that the writing helps me find up and down in what I can best describe as a combination of luck and desperation. And when all is said and done, maybe I just have to take things a little more relaxed. But I will stick to my decision of keeping my hands off of Liva and Judy. Similarly, Sabine will get all the attention she deserves. I should begin by going back to my bedroom and keep her warm.

Wednesday 3rd November, 2010

Dream Talk

Today I have stayed at home. It isn't particularly busy at the office, and I felt more need to be alone. It was nice to sleep in, especially now that the mornings are getting darker and I could have my morning coffee just by myself, all the girls were out. After my run and a light lunch I sat for hours and drank tea while I alternately stared into the air and watched the clouds floating quietly past my windows.

Can I honestly say that I also love Judy and Liva? As for Judy, it is not love in the same form as with Liva. And the love I feel for Liva is not the same as with Sabine. Perhaps there are several different kinds of love? I think so, but Judy is in a category by herself, and that is more about desire and lust than actual love. At best, a sort of love at first sight, but it is also more in the direction of pure fascination. I would not characterize my impressions of Karla as love, although she was an amazing sight. It takes more.

There has also been more of Judy than I had with Karla, but it still isn't love. As of yet, because it could possibly evolve into even more if circumstances were different. If, for instance, we had talked more and not only had fun mixed with flirtation. It is clearly an important detail with Sabine that we also have the intellectual ties.

Meanwhile, Judy is so delicious and so flirtatious, that I probably always would be a little wary when there were other men around. And without a basic trust, I have a hard time obtaining the important confidentiality.

My love for Liva is on another level. We have loved each other from the first, tentative stage where it was infatuation. After that came the growing dependence on each other's company and accompanying sense of cohesion. We got on excellently for a long time. At that stage I think we built up a loyalty that lasts a lifetime, even when our roads separated later. The fact that we have now, in a new period, been close to each other again reinforces my belief in the familial love, one has for parents and siblings in many cases. A third, and probably even stronger form of love may be the one people talk about regarding their children. I have not experienced it and never will. The responsibility is simply too great, and I'm getting too old to do without my sleep. Every time I see Nikolai, I remember that my decision to remain childless is correct even despite his stories, which confirm the complete and uncompromising love.

It must be because I am moving from phase one to phase two with Sabine, that I am so dramatically concerned with the risk of hurting her. I sincerely wish that we can build up our relationship and am ready to accept the inherent risk of losing if I can just convince her that I want her one hundred percent.

In the middle of all these considerations, Judy came home. I did not know where she had been, but was happy to see her. She came up to me on the windowsill and gave me a hug.

- You seem to be sad. Is something wrong?

- Hmm. Well. I sometimes think too much. And on days like this, when I have the opportunity to philosophize freely, my brain tends to boil over.

- What are you saying? What happens in your brain ...?

- Sorry. It's just that I cannot figure out how best to tell Sabine how much she means to me.

- She knows already. We still talk as very close friends. You have made a big impression on her, believe me.

- You haven't told her about the two of us, have you?

- No, don't worry. We've shared men before, but none of us has been emotionally involved with them. It is different with you and her. But I could not resist you and have always been aware that it did not change your feelings for Sabine.

- Thank you. And you are absolutely right. To me, the two of us had some amazing experiences, and it has not affected my longer-term intentions with Sabine. I would love to hold on to her for a long time.

- You can try out some dream-talking, perhaps?

- What do you mean?

I remembered that Sabine had referred to Judy as a dream-girl one of the first times she spoke of her. What was that really about?

- When I was a child my grandmother taught me some techniques, she was a kind of shaman - you know what it is?

- Something spiritual?

- Yes, among other things. She taught me how she could give me a lot of wisdom, without me needing to read a whole bunch of books. It's about communicating between two individuals' subconscious while you sleep.

Judy began to explain to me how I could try out dream-talk, or dream-conversation, to use a slightly better word. First and foremost, it is important to fall asleep in a relaxed and safe environment. It is not necessary to arrange a meeting in the shared dream, but the principle is that one party emerges in the other's dream. As far as I interpret it, the idea is that you can visit the other person's subconscious, but I understood the concept. Judy told me how her grandmother had gone to sleep with the little Judy lying back against her chest – what we popularly call the spoon sleeping position. She had told Judy to think about nothing and just breathe smoothly and deeply. Then Grandma started to synchronize her own breathing and concentrated on adapting her pulse and, as Judy put it, the brain waves. She probably meant the brain's electrical activity and change in frequencies. I was all ears!

She paused briefly and I could see how she got tears in her eyes from the memory.

- The first time I met Grandma in a dream, I got a little scared because she did not resemble herself. But she reassured me and told me that I would be totally safe, she would look after me. Actually that was not something she said, more like a sort of emotional or mental condition, which she was able to transfer to me. I was so young that I could not describe it in words at the time.

I was very moved to hear such a report, and I avoided expressing my otherwise skeptical attitude. It was all very fascinating, and I could see that it wasn't something Judy just invented.

Over a few years she had learned to receive her grandmother's knowledge, and that is why she is locally called the dream-girl as an adult. Not that she practiced it as some kind of witch, but she has used her skills as a quite alternatively trained psychologist. In fact that was what she was currently doing with me. Telling me how I can communicate with Sabine on another level.

- But there are two things you should remember. You can't be sure of visually recognizing Sabine, even if you are successful in joining her dream. Do not be confused, because you will not be in doubt that it is her. The second thing is, that you should not use your energy to speak or formulate what you say to her. As I have explained, this is more about a completely different exchange of emotions. But the effect is even better because it cannot be misunderstood.

- And she cannot read my mind?

- No. This is quite different. But if you are unsure of your feelings for her, you cannot hide anything. There is no filter.

I was a little dizzy at Judy's suggestion, but also grateful and touched that she had shared her knowledge. And she really wanted me to convince Sabine about my love in the purest way. I gave her a very long and heartfelt hug, and for the first time I could hold her close without thinking about where it might lead us. This was bigger.

Tonight, when Sabine come home and we've eaten, I will follow Judy's advice and lure Sabine to bed early. As I understand, it might be a good prelude to offer a massage during which I can begin my sync with her breathing and pulse. It is best to avoid sex to keep focus, but according to Judy, I should just stay away from the erogenous zones. This could be a problem with Sabine, my experience so far shows that she can be turned on by touch almost anywhere. But I can always try to think more about breathing. At least try.

She should be coming home soon. It's now almost half past five and we've agreed that this is the deadline to be part of a joint evening meal. Liva came home just a few minutes ago and it's so nice when we are all at the table.

Aha. There I heard the door again, so it's time to get in the kitchen and see what we can knock up from the contents of a refrigerator, which is fortunately better stocked now than when I lived by myself.

Thursday 4th November, 2010

Clarity

Last night I had the most wonderful dream, and it was one of those I will remember for the rest of my life.

Both the prelude and the experience was so bizarre that I could not get myself to bring it up when I arrived at Robert's, who had once more spontaneously invited me over to share a bottle of red wine. This time he had promised to cook as well, a meal of superbly baked pork tenderloin, which is one of his favorites. I could understand that he also needed a little man-to-man, so it suited me fine with a little diversion on top of my mystical journey into dream mysteries. All day at work I had found myself in a state of sober hangover, and I was in need of a little change, preferably with a culinary touch.

He is actually a good cook when he makes a little effort. It is perhaps somewhat traditional, but that kind of menu can also have its advantages. Potatoes baked in cream, a green salad and the most tender meat wrapped in puff pastry. Old days in new surroundings.

- It's great you take the effort to cook such a meal just for the two of us. Cheers!

- Only the best is good enough for us. And I thought I could probably lure you over here with a traditional dish on my menu.

- Absolutely. At any time. How are things with your dating, have you been busy out in the market?

- Yes, exactly. And the reason to invite you over. I would like to hear a little about your own experiences, because I'm in a bit of a dilemma.

- Okay, but I was not even on that many dates when it comes down to it. I fell for Sabine very quickly and have stopped my further search.

- But you did get to meet a few didn't you?

- Yeah, but no more than you can count on one hand. What happened to you?

I could not quite guess what his problem was. He had probably been on a lot more dates than I, and certainly taken them beyond a meeting at a café. Although he may be picky, he is an alpha-male who just has to go the whole way.

- I don't really know. But after hearing about your idea on having multiple, simultaneous relationships, I became a little unsure. And more curious to hear how you work it out.

- First tell me who you've met. Then I might be able to give input.

He was not aware that my model ultimately had not worked according to my original intention, but I would like to help.

- There have been many and a variety. But one of them is absolutely fantastic. She is divinely beautiful like Judy, I met at your party. We have met every Tuesday for heavenly sex during the last couple of weeks, but I cannot quite get a grip on whether she is something to bet on.

- Aha. An exotic type who radiates sensuality?

- Very much so. She is positively oozing sex!

- What is making you unsure, then?

- Well, she insists that we always meet here at my place. And she has demands on very specific times. Fortunately, I can comply, but it's a little strange that she can never stay a little longer.

- She may be married and needs to go home to her husband?

- I don't know. I haven't asked her. The only thing I know about her life is that she has a clothing shop up north of Copenhagen. And she dresses in clothes that she has designed herself.

It suddenly occurred to me that Robert was most likely hijacked by Karla.

- Is her name Karla?

- Ehm, yes. Do you know her?

- Hahaha. Not really, but she caught me, too, when I had an online profile. We met at Theodor's and I was ready to invite her home after five seconds. She is, as you say, a pure Aphrodite – but I found out that she is married and has a son. Not only that, but she is obviously out in the city to cultivate a hobby in being unfaithful to her husband.

- How did you find out?

- Her husband rang while we were having a cup of coffee. She told him, while I overheard the conversation, that she was out with some girlfriends. I lost my otherwise great appetite and dropped going forward. I didn't want to get involved with someone I initially know that I can't trust. She is beautiful, but dangerous. Do not let yourself be controlled by her.

Robert was quiet for a moment. I thought that at best it could be someone else than Karla, but there were too many matches and I did not want him to be trapped with hurt feelings.

- You may be right. It was precisely your experience of finding new women, I was curious about. That we have been captivated by not only the same type, but apparently the same woman just makes me more confident in my case. I will not see Karla again. She has been exciting, but there was something wrong all along.

He had felt it too. The otherwise imperceptible thing when a guy falls so fervently for a passionate and seductive woman. The small difference means that we as men can be so badly blinded. Women can do something special when seducing, we men never master, but if we learn to share our experiences, we might get wiser? In any event it was a pleasure to see Robert lighten up. I was sorry that he lost its Tuesday-mistress there and then, but glad that he was wiser.

Thanks to my talk with him, I too had learned something about my own future. I will not be dragged around in the ring by my women. They have controlled too much, and if it continues, I lose my self-respect. Interestingly, the advice given to a good friend can provide a very clear self-insight. Sometimes things need to be said out loud and not just thought over.

Robert gave me a proper bear-hug when I had emptied the last glass of wine and chose to go home. When it came down to it, I did not need to tell him about my own recent experiences regarding everything with women. But on the walk back to my apartment, memories of last night came back.

Sabine had been tired after a long day of lectures and writings, so she was easy to persuade into a massage in bed. I began to soften her shoulders as she lay on her stomach with her arms spread up against the headboard. I softly massaged each of her arms all the way out to the hands, and I laid myself gently on her back while I kissed her now relaxed shoulders. I inhaled her wonderful scent and sniffed deeply along both sides of her neck and under the soft hair.

Our breathing began to be as one and I moved my fingers along her spine and lower back. With symmetrical and circular motions, I tried to influence her energies, so they moved toward her heart. Her pulse and respiration increased with my own, and it was easy to find the shared rhythm. I remembered Judy's warning about staying away from specially erogenous zones and sat down at her feet to give her unauthorized reflexology. After a while I could not help but to treat her legs and with our now shared rising pulse and breathing, I came to the inside of her thighs. I simply could not keep myself away from the most erogenous zones anymore. By now Judy's warnings didn't matter. Sabine was as turned on as ever.

It felt like I was one with her when she came. I could feel the same as she, but in a different way. But it was like we experienced a single explosion of cohesion there and then. I kissed her again and again all over while I once more synchronized our slowly decreasing breathing and pulse.

I have no idea when or how I suddenly floated in front of the smiling angel who caressed my cheek with her soft touch. Her right hand slid down and met my left, and I grabbed it. She pulled me forward, while she in some strange way slid backwards. Our movement was like floating in a mixture of water and oil, without being parted. I looked up and saw a sky which instead of being full of clouds gave me an impression of flying high over a landscape. But at the same time I knew that we had just taken off from a sort of gravity, because otherwise we would not fly and experience weightlessness. I was slightly confused about the combined fear of height and the feeling of being in complete balance with the elements. My traveling companion gave me peace of mind without words, yet it was as though I could hear a phrase.

- Do not worry. It really is us, and we have nothing to fear.

As Judy had told me, I could not recognize Sabine, but I was in no doubt that it was she who held my hand on this trip. I felt more than heard her reassuring and affirmative thoughts.

However, it was extremely disturbing to recognize my own skepticism about such an experience and be aware of it at the same time. Was I aware that it was a dream? Did I want to wake up? At the time I was not able to verify anything, but let myself go with her movements.

Then I remembered that this whole exercise was about me bringing her an assurance of my affection. I was indeed in her dream now. We were together in this and I should focus on showing her my innermost feelings. We were together and she could understand without words, if only I concentrated enough. But how could I tell her without going into further explanation? I tried to follow her movements, but also wanted to move myself into new directions. I was dizzy and the last thing I remember is that she smiled at me while everything around us faded into a light fog.

The real Sabine has not come home yet, though it is late this Thursday evening. I am satiated after dinner with Robert and mentally exhausted after the experiment, Judy lured me into. But it was great to wake up in the morning as Sabine came back from her morning shower and dressed herself here in the bedroom. I pretended that I was still sleeping, but enjoyed the sight of her quiet movements. She was probably also aware that I watched her, because she made an extra effort in getting dressed slowly.

When she was done she came over and sat on the edge of the bed and saw that I was awake. Her smile was as beautiful as in the dream.

- Thank you for the lovely trip, you joined me in.

- So it was not just a dream?

- No, but it was also a dream. There's just more in dreams than we normally experience. I learned this when I was in South America. And I am glad that we can do more together than I had hoped for.

- You are wonderful, Sabine.

- And I am also a student, so I have to leave now.

I was happy to kiss my girlfriend goodbye and look forward to a day where I did not have to do much other than check my emails and read today's news on various online media. After my compulsory running and late lunch, I got online and saw the invitation from Robert, and thanks to the perfectly ordinary evening with him, the world is beginning look like itself again. But I am tired as a retirement home and will go to bed early. Sabine has not even come home yet, but I need to sleep alone tonight.

One night without dreams would for a change be perfectly fine with me.

Friday 5th November, 2010

On Top Again

For once Nikolai seemed enthusiastic when we met at our favorite bar. No complaints or other dissatisfaction about daycare or new infections, so I could fairly quickly turn the conversation into the somewhat esoteric area.

- I had the strangest dream a couple of nights ago. It was as if I entered into the same dream that Sabine had. Have you ever tried something like that?

- Hmm. Once in a while I dream about other people, but usually is not anyone I know. Well, maybe a former girlfriend sometimes.

- I have tried that too, but this time it was extremely lifelike, and when Sabine woke me up yesterday morning, she thanked me for the dream. It was really strange.

- Have you talked to her any more about it?

- No, she was at the university all day yesterday and I was home alone and went to bed very early. This morning she was already up when I awoke. I slept like a log last night.

- It sounds strange. But I have stopped taking an interest in that kind of mysteries. Evolution is scarier.

- What do you mean?

- For example, a complex instrument like an eye is the result of millions of years of gradual improvement. The first living organisms were blind. How on earth does it work, that animals and humans have developed vision?

- You are just as strange as some of my dreams.

Nikolai sometimes brings up subjects he has been wondering about over a long period of time. Not unlike Benjamin, and perhaps they both have difficulty talking to their respective wives on such odd topics. The media often writes about couples not talking enough about feelings, but that is perhaps not the sole problem in communication between men and women. Imagine if you could be the proverbial fly on the wall and witness an evening's conversation between the ordinary, married couple. Maybe there will be no conversation at all in many homes?

- How are you doing anyway with all of your women? I found out at your party that your relationship with Sabine is no longer a secret to Liva.

- Yeah, you haven't even heard about that strange story.

I told him how Liva had known all along that Sabine was my girlfriend, but that they had spared me from having to explain it at first.

- Well, it's good that things worked out for you. Are you still living together all three of you or has Liva moved back to Xenia's father?

- We live together and Judy from the party is also a part of it now. So I've in fact got all my three women, what do you say about that? I actually think it's pretty cool.

- Haha. The same as from the beginning. You risk a hell of a lot of hassle.

Fortunately both of us could both see how hilarious the situation was, because my plan to find three women had evolved quite differently than intended. I hadn't exactly intended to be living with all three women. Nevertheless, they were now in my life and I dropped involving Nikolai in my concerns about hurting Sabine. The last few days I hadn't even cheated. It also seemed that both Liva and Judy realized that I mostly belonged to Sabine.

The rest of the evening with Nikolai included more talk about Darwin and the possible divine forces that could be an almost equally good explanation as natural selection. Nikolai told me that it wasn't even the strongest who survive according Darwin, but the ones best to adapt. And I might be a good example with all my women. We ended up somewhat intoxicated and I was glad to again have lent my bike to Sabine so I could walk home quietly and carefully a little after midnight.

On my journey through the city, Nikolai's words about selection and adaption made me think about my own choices. It seemed natural for me to live with all my women, but most correct to have only one girlfriend. There is still something in the genes, which is the result of many generations in steady relationships. As Elizabeth has touched on, the foundation is different now, and many people choose serial monogamy. But to keep a sort of modern harem is both inconvenient and dangerous. Nikolai is right about that.

Just the thought of last weekend makes me stressed. Of course it was exciting and rewarding to enjoy Liva and Judy, but in the long run, I can't live my life with a consistently bad conscience. Now that I have spoken to both of them about the conflicting feelings and been honest with both them and myself, I feel a lot better. It's liberating to be on top again and begin to regain my good old determination. This coming weekend will probably be nice, and I want to take the initiative to some new activities.

Maybe we could all go on some excursion together?

When I came home a little while ago, they had all gone to bed and I sat down to check online for something cultural to do tomorrow and on Sunday. The walk has sobered me up, and it is reassuring to become inspired by enjoyable activities for the next couple of days. It's great, too, that I've apparently learned to adapt myself to new surroundings.

Monday 8th November, 2010

Leader of the Pack

Dear Christian,

Where are your updates to the outskirts of Denmark? I have not heard from you since right after the holidays, and even then you were quite sparse with information about the women in your new life. You promised to keep me updated, and don't start saying that nothing has happened, because I know you, and I think you've involved yourself in a story that I don't want to miss out on.

Please find time to write back!

PS: I have suspended selling my house until after the winter, so if you and one or more female friends feel like an old-fashioned Christmas, you're welcome to spend it here. It will be by the book with homemade specialties.

Sincerely,

Marie

I can just see that happening. A Christmas at Marie's with all my women – I would become deaf inside the first hour with all the talking, I'm sure. But it was super nice to get the invitation. A bit cheeky to tell about it so far in advance, who makes plans so far ahead, and how does one gracefully say 'no' without having a conflicting appointment? Oh, she'll probably survive even if she is alone out there.

Dear Marie,

You sure get your invitations out early. It sounds very enticing to spend Christmas in the countryside, and I will mention it to "the women in my new life" as you call them. Lately I have had a full bingo. I now live not only with Sabine and Liva, but also a friend Sabine knows from

Argentina. Her name is Judy, she is one of the world's most beautiful creatures and should be listed in the thesaurus under exotic. She arrived just before the autumn break and apparently is in no hurry to continue on her journey around Europe.

Initially I was a little confused by suddenly being surrounded by three beautiful women, and it has not been without a few challenges. But I have learned incredibly much about myself in the process. I know that it is no use leaving out details to you, so you might as well get a few of the ones that you are asking for.

Of course I could not keep my fingers from Judy, she charmed and flirted herself right into my pants, literally speaking. In my defense and at the risk of sounding like a little boy, I must mention that she started it.

I was easy to persuade, and it was only after a few weeks with a lot more activity in my sex life than usual, that reality began to dawn on me. It dawned on me that I could not neglect my increasing bad conscience toward Sabine. Therefore, I had a talk first with Liva and then with Judy about all of it. In each their won way, I think they understood my dilemma, and in each their own way, they gave me good advice. I have yet to decide whether I should tell Sabine whole truth, but I focus on her now. She is my girlfriend.

Our weekdays are working fine and you would enjoy the atmosphere we have at the table when we regularly all have dinner together. I have no idea how long Judy intend to stay and Liva is bound to either to move back to Mick or find something else. But until now I thrive as the famous, proud rooster in the hen house.

PS: Sorry that it took me so long to write, good of you to remind me.

Sincerely,

Christian

I went into the shared kitchen at the office and fetched more coffee before I found myself embarking on the more business-oriented emails. The most important was from a potential customer, who unfortunately wouldn't sign up, although they had received a really sensible offer. But it took more to depress me today because the weekend has been beyond all expectations.

Saturday morning I was up first and filled a couple of large bakery bags down at the organic. The scent of freshly brewed coffee gradually got the girls into the kitchen and I suggested that we should take a trip to the Louisiana Museum. Especially Judy liked the idea.

- It is always exciting to see how art is disseminated in different countries.

- Yes, and you also seemed quite excited about our visit at the Glyptotek, Liva said.

I choked on a piece of bread and had to empty a large glass of juice. Sabine looked at me, concerned, but I signaled that everything was OK.

After that little interlude, we agreed that an afternoon of arts and culture was just what we needed. This time I wanted to keep the flock together, so there were no temptations or diversions. But as far as I remembered, Louisiana is built for guests to walk from one end to another.

That turned out to still be the case, and the trip proceeded without drama. I felt as the leader of a wonderful family, although the composition was at least as controversial as a part of the exhibited works. We had a late lunch at their café and eagerly exchanged our thoughts and opinions about everything from Andy Warhol to Per Kirkeby. We disagreed on a lot, but that just made the discussion more interesting. My women are smart, beautiful and spectacular. I've won in the lottery of life.

Saturday evening we saw a film that Sabine needed to watch for a course, and I ended up falling asleep on the sofa. They laughed and called me an old, tired man. They could be right, because I had no trouble staying in bed almost the entire Sunday, but the cause was not old age, on the contrary, because Sabine makes me feel like a teenager again.

Later in the day, Liva and Judy succeeded to lure us on a tour of the King's Gardens, but after a little while in the cold, we would all rather return home for hot chocolate. I found out that I sometimes miss the intimate experiences with Liva and Judy, but now I had been faithful for a week without problems.

The most damaging effect of being surrounded by three women is that I spend so much time thinking about them. Today at the office, for instance, I have not been doing anything besides writing to Marie. Most of the time I have been daydreaming and wondering how the future will evolve. To me, it's alright if Judy stays. I suppose we can occasionally enjoy each other without that causing problems? Liva is welcome to stay with Xenia as well. And she will be welcome to come home early when the child is ill and would rather sleep at home than in the kindergarten. There are many opportunities to get everything in place, if

I'm just thinking long term and not running amok in the candy store.

I'm a man, after all, and it is prudent to be somewhat strategic.

I previously wrote to Marie, that my focus is solely on Sabine and this now strikes me as comical. I wonder if she sees through me and comes to the same conclusion as I do? What the heck, you make choices until you get better ideas.

It's about time to close down for the day, and I almost believe that I can already smell my women and their wonderful skills at home in my kitchen. Hunger makes my stomach rumble and I want to go home.

Tuesday 9th November, 2010

Home Alone

When I came home from the office today, I was amazed at how quiet my apartment was. In stark contrast to Monday evening, where I was greeted by exactly the scents, I had hoped for: beautiful women, curry and coriander. The girls had decided to experiment with the best of the East, and they conjured a delightful meal of rice, chicken, vegetables and spices.

After we had set ourselves at the table, I almost wanted to say a prayer for all the things I was grateful of, but kept it to myself and proposed a toast instead.

- I am so glad that you have all enriched my life with your company. Cheers to you, the best women in the world!

- Wow, you almost have tears in your eyes, Liva said.

- Yes, and your voice is almost breaking, Sabine added.

I was very touched. Here they all sat. My original soul mate, the super exotic Judy and the young and forever flourishing Sabine. It was hard to find words to describe my happiness, but Judy got me down to earth again with her wonderful sense of the moment.

- Maybe you'd better pass around the dishes instead of becoming too ... what's the word ... solemn?

We ate until we were about to crack. They had prepared a royal meal, and I enjoyed every mouthful as much as listening to the exchange of stories about their different experiences during the day.

Sabine had been through a few lectures dealing with gender roles in the series of James Bond movies, and we all came up with good scenes, we could remember. The conversation inspired us to reserve next weekend for watching our favorites, and I look forward to that already.

At Liva's work they had begun a new round of layoffs, and she talked about how it affected the mood out there. It's never fun to know that either yourself are at risk of being fired or knowing that next month there's a small handful fewer colleagues. We tried to encourage her and look on the bright side. Sometimes a new job may be a breath of fresh air and a boost for the career. She admitted, too, that she has an online job agent running and has already applied for a few jobs. I am quite sure that she can easily find something else, and she has not exactly praised her current job, so I cross my fingers and hope for the best.

Judy had walked around town at random and had been all the way to Vesterbro and through both Norrebro and Frederiksberg. It made a big impression on her how different our neighborhoods are both regarding architecture and the people she met on the streets. Copenhagen is a very small town compared to Buenos Aires, but it does offer a big diversity within short distances. She thought that we might as well call our own capital city Buenos Aires because it's constantly so windy here. I had to explain to Liva and Sabine that the name directly translated from Spanish means "good winds". They understood the pun, but had never thought about it. However, the winds are probably better, or at least more comfortable down in northern Argentina, than here in Copenhagen during November.

During our talk, I repeatedly felt a lump in my throat by the lucky change my life had undergone. Admittedly, it was Elizabeth's challenge and good-natured teasing that kick-started my new adventure, but as time had passed and I inadvertently ended up here, the god or goddess of fortune had been extremely generous.

And now I sit here all alone a Tuesday evening. When I got home, there was a handwritten note on the kitchen table from Sabine. She has gone to the movies with Judy and Liva to catch a movie, they did not expect would be of interest to me. Xenia is at the babysitter, and I was just to heat some remnants from yesterday's banquet and enjoy myself with an evening without obligations.

Without obligations? It was not that I saw either her or the others as an obligation. Actually I would rather consider them as my new dependencies if one can use the word in this sense. I was briefly quite restless and irritable because they once again took control, but found peace over a few glasses of red wine. Watched the news on television and followed Sabine's recommendation to eat leftovers from yesterday. But something was missing. I lacked the good company. They may be right that I wasn't in the target group for their choice of movies, but I am so much the target for their sociability.

Am I experiencing a hint of jealousy? That my three women chose each other's company without me for a single evening should not make me uncomfortable and I am not nervous about whether they are sharing their experiences. Or maybe

I'm slightly worried that Sabine gets too many details, but it is more the feeling of missing them all, that I struggle with here on my very-home-alone evening.

I start thinking about how Ulrich once told that when he was on a week-long seminar, he missed his children so much, he just wanted to go home. Maybe I should have a talk with him about missing?

Hi Ulrich,
How about meeting for dinner somewhere in town tomorrow? I can't remember if it's your week with the kids, but I would like to talk to you about some things that have affected me recently. It is indeed on a rudely short notice, but I hope you have time. We could meet at the anchor in Nyhavn and grab a beer before moving on to the excellent restaurant Salt at the Admiral Hotel. It is not exactly a discount place, but it's on me!
Let me know,
Christian

I hope he doesn't have the kids and that he will accept my invitation. His economy is in no shape for expensive restaurants, but I know he will enjoy a sublime meal. If I'm lucky, he has no new escapades to tell about himself. And I would appreciate to hear his input to my frustrations.

Wednesday 10th November, 2010

Loving More than One

On my way across Kongens Nytorv I noticed Ulrich driving in his car looking for a parking space. I waved and walked toward the anchor. It was impossible to say where he might get lucky to park his car around here.

After a few minutes he walked up from behind, so he must have found a vacanct spot at St. Annae Square. Cars and Copenhagen do not mix well and I am happy to get around mostly on foot and by bicycle.

We went down along Nyhavn and remembered the many summers spent there looking at tourists and scantily clad women. This evening was somewhat more quiet and dark, but there's always a nice atmosphere there. It also helped that Ulrich was nicely relaxed. He is much more in balance after his soon to be ex-wife, Karen, moved out, and it is clear that his life no longer contains the stress factors entailed by a failing marriage.

- It must be nice for you to finally be moving on separately.

- You better believe that I enjoy it. And we are quite good at the practicalities of having the kids every other week. Recently, Karen had an appointment and asked if I could have them an evening outside the normal schedule, and it was just a pleasure for me. She came by with all three of them, and a whole pile of laundry. Haha.

- Oh no, are you saying that she makes you do her laundry?

- Well, she doesn't have a washing machine in her new apartment.

- But still. I honestly think that's wrong. Don't you feel she's taking advantage of you?

- I just help where I can.

Some things never change. He has the same gene as I – we cannot say no, and it was perhaps not so different from having Liva live at my place.

- You're being exploited a bit by Liva yourself, aren't you?

- Hehe. Yeah. I was thinking the same thing. Sorry. I didn't mean to criticize.

- How is everything going in your circus of women, anyway?

I told him that his theory had been correct. Liva knew from the start that Sabine and I were lovers. He laughed heartily at that. We had not been talking much at the party because I was so busy mingling around and waiting on everybody. But he had not forgotten Judy.

- That girl from Argentina, Sabine's friend – she really was a beauty. It was a shame I didn't get to know her better. And when we continued at the Park Café, she was suddenly gone.

- Yes, she said it was hard for her to follow conversations with all the loud music.

Should I tell him what had happened when she came home to me sitting in the dark kitchen after the party? It was an essential part of everything I wanted to talk to him about. At the same time, I mostly wanted to keep some details about both Liva and Judy a little secret so it would not sound too bragging. Even between two such good friends as Ulrich and me there is a small taboo for me. Maybe because I long ago became involved with a girl he had just broken up with. Now he was alone and I have my three women – no reason to boast too much.

Instead I chose a somewhat neutral angle and began to talk about love and missing more generally. He has three children whom he loves more than anything on earth, and I have three women that make me happy. Whether it is comparable, I cannot say, but he seemed to follow my thoughts.

- OK, let me just make it absolutely clear. So now you live with all three of them and you're Sabine's boyfriend. Have you never been tempted by Judy?

- Yes, certainly. For that matter, by Liva as well. That's my whole point. Do you think it's possible to love three women at the same time? A bit the same way as you love all your three children, I mean.

- That's different. Love for one's children is something else entirely. You might not understand it as you have chosen life without children, but let me tell you ... The fully unconditional love I have for the kids is on another level than anything I have experienced.

He's probably right. But it was nice to have talked it over. It had put everything into perspective and I was glad that it was not necessary with all the details. This is about principles, and his response was reasonable. If he knew that I had been with them all, he would be distracted from the main point: The joy of three women simultaneously, and missing them when they are not there.

The feeling of yearning and longing is universal, and he also admitted that he still misses the safety of being part of a traditional family. I almost think he would take Karen back if she asked for it. So much easier than finding a new girlfriend who should even take on the role as an extra mother. But I hope for him that they both move forward and don't try again. They would too easily fall back into their roles, small and large differences would flare up, and I think the kids would feel insecure.

We finished off with a couple of strong cups of espresso and I had more peace of mind about my feelings. It is normal to miss someone, you love. It is okay to love more than just one. Although it was my own conclusion, and possibly reached by suspicious, even selfish motives, I was more settled. He offered to drive me home, and now I sit here peacefully and look forward to lie down next to my beautiful girlfriend. Knowing that I can get up tomorrow and be among the world's three most beautiful women makes me smile from the inside out.

Thursday 11th November, 2010

A New Twist

Happiness can indeed be capricious. Now I had finally, after careful consideration, found that I could live out my version of Elizabeth's model. It could work even though, or perhaps because, all four of us lived together. I had them all close in my life, and it suited me perfectly to have the prospect of living out a little extra adventure just once in a while. In everyday life, I have no problem with keeping my faithfulness toward Sabine. And then suddenly Judy announces that she'll be leaving. What is the purpose of that?

Instead of having realized the most likely development and getting accustomed to the idea that her stay is temporary, I've been solving my puzzle so I could get the best out of the excitement. This is damned annoying. But also stupid of me, upon reflection, as it was inevitable that she would eventually leave. Why had I not taken advantage of a few more situations, and enjoyed more of her, while there was still time? Typically for me I had been thinking too much and had tried to solve a problem on quite the wrong basis, and it eventually resulted in this virtual slap in the face. I could really beat myself for my naivety.

The news came about during dinner when we all sat and talked. Liva had been telling us a little more about the firings at her job, and Sabine about some articles they had analyzed at the university, when I asked Judy about her day.

- Oh, I've seen enough of your beautiful city now, I think. It's time to move on to my other friends in Paris and Zurich.

- What? Already? I exclaimed with a little too high vocal pitch.

Sabine and Liva looked a bit surprised at my reaction. But they hadn't had the challenge of my puzzle.

- We have known all the time that Judy had to travel on. Actually, she has been here longer than planned, Sabine said.

Obviously Sabine was the one most prepared that Judy was only here on a sort of extended holiday. And I would think that Liva hadn't given it much thought in the middle of the problems of being in a insecure position.

- One thing I don't fully understand, Judy: Why have you chosen to visit Europe here at the darkest and coldest time of the year? Liva asked, so she had given it some thought. Curiously in the same area as myself at the beginning of Judy's visit.

- That's simple to explain. I have been living the most of my life in almost just one season. For me it is exciting to experience something completely different. On the journey down through Germany and France, I look forward to see the winter set in. And in Switzerland I will surely try to go skiing.

Personally I would rather see her on water skis at any time, but even that would probably remain a fantasy. Damn it all!

With a little luck there may still be a chance to find her home alone, because it is not until this coming Thursday that she has a ticket from the Central Station toward south. A new

222

puzzle began to take shape in my head. While I saw the days ahead of me and time running out, the girls talked more about everything Judy must remember to experience especially in Paris. To soothe my mind, I offered to clean the kitchen and made an effort to hide my disappointment. I miss her already and got a sinking feeling of longing.

Now I'm checking my calendar for the coming week with the pleasant background sound of girls chatting about sights in Paris. Will it be the same to hear only Sabine and Liva sit and socialize in the living room? No, I would be missing something. They fit so well here, all of them. And they're great together. But I cannot offer Judy work and I have no way of influencing her decision. When can I plan one last time for a proper goodbye?

Tomorrow I am going out with the guys, and I also have appointments for the first three days of next week. And then it's Thursday. Damn it. Couldn't she have given me some more time, so there was room for just a little planning? Show a little respect, woman!

During the weekend, perhaps? We had talked about reserving it for the James Bond character and watch a bunch of the best from the series. This means that we are all going to be home and I cannot possibly sneak myself into Judy's room at night. It looks increasingly hopeless, and I can feel a sense of panic spreading as I realize that I've missed the last chance.

It seriously pisses me off that I as late as yesterday evening claimed to have everything under control. Everything looked perfect, and then something happens unexpectedly. If I had just realized that Judy was obviously a temporary pleasure, I could have acted differently. Would I have? If I had been going full speed and not been over-pondering, I had perhaps been more stressed out over my conscience. There was also the unpleasant, yet exciting risk that Sabine discovered something. Maybe I've done the right thing, but it irks me that Judy disappears out of my life.

The idea of breaking completely out of my life and join her traveling strikes me for a moment, but that would be absurd. I love Sabine. Perhaps we can entice Judy to come visit us next summer so she can experience Denmark in the most beautiful season. Or we can visit her back in Argentina. I cannot accept if I never get to see Judy again.

And she is sitting right there in my living room. Reason triumphs, or maybe it's a split victory with emotions. How difficult can it be to go fetch a bottle of champagne and join the girls to propose an early bon voyage-toast?

It would be appropriate, and I have to get used to the idea that Judy has been a fantastic part of my project. Actually, for a short time I've succeeded to live with my three women. I would just really like to have more of it!

Friday the 12th November, 2010

Focusing on Two

Daniel and Mikkel sat and talked, when I showed up to our after-hours beer appointment. They were in the middle of some complicated, technical hullabaloo going over my head, so I went up to the bar to get a round. This evening, it appeared to be Kasper, who was not there – no one knew why, but that's the way he sometimes is.

While I stood waiting for the beers, I thought a little about how it was often easier to conduct a conversation, when there were just three of us. A subject could easily be fully discussed and there were no interruptions or two ongoing, simultaneous discussions. When we're together, all four of us, we usually talk in pairs, and with my curiosity, I cannot help but listen to both conversations. The result is an obviously decreased concentration in both subjects and a superficial participation. It is not because I prefer that one of my friends don't show up – nor something I've really given much thought in the past. But my current situation with women gives perspective.

When Judy travels on, could it be that I can focus on Liva and Judy more easily? I need all the positive side-effects, I can find. But it is different at home than being out with friends. At home I can sit and listen without participating quite so actively when the girls talk. If I'm too passive in the company of the gentlemen Daniel, Mikkel and Kasper, they just think that I have problems or am being bored. There are obviously many differences and nuances in the way I communicate with women and men, even when it happens in a larger group.

I thoughtfully returned to our table and they could both immediately see that my thoughts were elsewhere.

- Is something wrong? You look a little distracted.

Mikkel had not been there when we last met, and he still needed to hear about the latest developments of my project.

- Well. Until recently I thought that I'd been successful with all my three women. You know that I quite quickly got both Sabine and Liva as roommates, and since the party Judy has also been living with us.

- So what is wrong?

- Yesterday Judy said that she will be leaving next week. And I had just come to a conclusion that I could handle all the temptations. Sabine is my girlfriend, but it's also wonderful to have Liva and Judy so close.

- Oh, come on! It wouldn't take more than a few weeks for you to sidetrack and risk losing it all.

- Oh, thanks for the confidence.

- Well, Mikkel has a point. Do you really think that you could keep yourself from Judy?

- I am convinced. You won't believe how much I've thought it all through: Pros, cons, temptation and disaster. On the whole, the past few weeks have been rather turbulent. But super exciting and it gave me a good insight into some aspects of myself I did not know.

I told them about our cultural excursions and how our unwritten rules on joint dinner worked. How I enjoyed coming home to an apartment that was full of life in contrast to earlier. And how it dawned on me the other day when they all went out that I missed them dearly.

- But you have always been pretty fond of your own company and not least peace and quiet?

- Yes, I was surprised at first, too. Maybe I am getting old and sentimental.

- Well, you still have two out of three. That's better than none, isn't it?

- Well, sure it is. And deep down I also knew that Judy was only here temporarily. But it has been so wonderful with all three, although it ended up being short lived.

They did their best to cheer me up and I was quite touched by their compassion. In a way, they could easily have called it a luxury problem, but maybe they also found out it was nice to talk about more than technical stuff for a change. After a few more beers, however, I chose to go home.

It's only two days ago that my conversation with Ulrich helped me get the pieces to fall into place. Now I sit here feeling ashamed that I cannot be satisfied with two of the three women inside the living room. They could feel my altered state of mind as well when I got home, but they let me get some time alone at the computer. The feeling of being part of all of them gives me a comfort, a bit like when I as a child fell asleep while I could hear my parents sit and talk in our living room. Despite a good number of years as a single, there is obviously still something below the surface, which I had just ignored or suppressed. Daniel is very right in saying that I normally thrive in my own company, but that was before I tried this model which could be the answer to new relationships structures. I've probably been a little too optimistic.

I could obviously resume the hunt for a replacement for Judy, but it would be totally wrong against Sabine. Things were different when I first created my online dating profile, and I've just been incredibly lucky that Judy ever became the third woman.

The thoughts from before about falling asleep to the muffled conversation from the living room and revive my childhood comfort brings other strange thoughts to mind. I rarely think of my childhood and in no way do I wish to be a child again. Not that those were unhappy years, or that I lacked love. But something gives me a lump in my throat. Why does love always involve the grief of losing?

I wonder what they're talking about for such a long time in there? I'm not in the mood to figure it out, but I hope that Sabine soon wants to go to bed. I have so much need for her closeness tonight.

Monday 15th November, 2010

A Positive Angle

- So then, are you getting a lot of Nyataimori these days?

William and I were enjoying sushi for dinner, and of course he was referring to the weird tradition of serving raw fish on naked women.

- Hehe. Oh no, I prefer my women au naturel.

- Don't mix food and women?

- Now that you mention it, I really like it when we're all at home for dinner. It is the highlight of the day, when I sit and enjoy their company in the evening. I hadn't imagined how much it could mean to me.

- That's the way I've felt for years. Ever since I became a father it's the time at home with the family that makes life worth living. The fact that you are trying out a somewhat different model is just cool.

I was yet to inform him of the small detail that my model had cracked.

- Unfortunately it isn't quite so successful anymore.

- Why not? What happened?

- Judy is leaving on Thursday. I should have prepared myself for it but I was so enticed by all three of them that I spent all my energy curbing my desires. Excuse my directness, but both Judy and Liva are hard to resist.

- And soon you're left with only two women in your life? You poor guy.

William could be sarcastic in a good way, and he had every possible right to tease me. It was crazy of me to complain and I was glad that he took me seriously in his own way.

- No, I know. I should not complain, but lately I've been feeling almost schizophrenic. I am and have been, all high with happiness, and at the same time I can become so terribly angry that Judy will soon be gone. They should all be a part of my life, I think.

- You cannot eat your cake and have it, too.

- Oh. I've heard that one before and thought that I could disprove the case. For instance, we just had a weekend where everything worked perfectly.

It all began Saturday morning with a solid breakfast of scrambled eggs and bacon with fried tomatoes on toasted rye bread... This combination was Judy's new favorite dish, and we all agreed it was a good combo. While we ate, we agreed that the smartest plan for our James Bond weekend would be to buy the whole box set. Then we would take turns choosing two films each. One would be the favorite, and the second would be what each of us perceived as the most ridiculous. It was not allowed to comment on the films we chose, but afterward we would tell about the background to our selections.

I was hoping that Sabine and Liva would go out and buy the movies, so maybe I could get some time alone with Judy, but Liva and I ended up staying at home and preparing various appetizers while the others got the movies. It was inevitable that Octopussy would be among the selections, so it was obvious to make a dish of fried squid with tzatiki. Caviar and champagne were also inescapable, and of course we were stocked up on gin, vodka and martini.

It was very appropriate that we had already had scrambled eggs, so we decided to serve steaks for dinner. That should fit any of the eight movies during the weekend.

William was very astonished when I told more about our James Bond weekend.

- Did you really watch eight movies in two days?

- Yes, it was quite intense. But nice and cozy, too!

He was curious to hear more about how I tackled the move from being single to having three women. And that I a few days from now would be in decline. William remains a best friend. There is no competition, but an empathetic interest in knowing I am happy in my life. It's probably thanks to his own safe family life that he's so good to talk to.

I told him that I had no choice. Judy had to travel on and I could do nothing about it. It was too late and wrong to find a replacement for 'the exoticĒ, but I had, for a short time, achieved my goal. This weekend I had come to a new conclusion that I would look back on the past month as a period I will never forget. Even if I don't get more adventures with Judy, no one can take the memories away from me. And I can live on with a fairly good conscience.

I see my way of tackling the new development as evidence that I can adapt again – it's always about finding a positive angle.

Sabine and I almost had square eyes when we went to bed late last night, and we only just managed to say goodnight before we fell into a deep sleep. We didn't meet in our dreams, but I am sure that they involved car chases as well as heavy intakes of dry martinis for both of us – shaken, not stirred.
I didn't focus on synchronizing my breathing with her, but it was her I would protect when I was in the second world defeating enemies. Whether or not I was the hero she was rescued by, I could not say, but here in the late Monday evening as she lies sleeping again, I would like to think I am her hero. She went to bed early tonight, and I'm tempted to wake her in a few seconds when I accompany her under the duvet. She is my Vesper: *Once you've tasted it, that's all you want to drink.*

Tuesday 16th November, 2010

At Ease

Dear Christian,

You do not need to decide anything about Christmas in the countryside yet, but I wanted to give you the option. We can always get back to that.

Thanks for your voluminous report and congratulations that you managed everything with your three women. You always seem to find solutions to even the most difficult challenge, but I am still impressed and surprised by this. If I were to give you a little advice, I would recommend that you do not tell Sabine about your digression. And for God's sake make sure you control yourself. The whole thing can explode when you all live together. It would be different if you had three mistresses in town, so be wise. Are you sure that your model can work in the longer term? Had it been me, I had chosen to keep things separate, which I actually have practiced successfully on several occasions. At the moment that the side of my life is dormant, and that is also one of the reasons why I yearn for Copenhagen. There's nothing going on here.

Sincerely,

Marie

It must be tough on her patience to sit out there in the countryside and wait for an upturn in the housing market. But it's a good thing she can act as a psychologist for me during the dark and long nights. I could invite her to spend Christmas here in Copenhagen but she says we don't need to arrange anything concrete yet. Christmas is still a way off, and many things can change overnight. I have learned a thing or two about that during autumn.

Dear Marie,

Lower the price and come back! No, sorry. I shouldn't stress you when you are being so nice and praise me. Your advice is always good and I had also arrived at the conclusion that Sabine doesn't need to hear about everything. The day after tomorrow, I will have one problem less, because Judy is leaving. I've been in two minds whether it would be an idea to plan one last time with her, but you're right. When I have been lucky so far, it would be too stupid to ruin everything for a single bang.

Besides, my initial thought was not that I would be living with three women, but as things evolved, it happened almost by itself. Whether it had been easier having multiple relationships going under more traditional conditions, I cannot say. I had probably been just as stressful if I had to coordinate that and I would have missed the many pleasant evenings we have all spent together. So I regret nothing, but I am annoyed at the fact that Judy leaves.

Love

Christian

Marie's email got me thinking that Elizabeth had warned as well me in her mail a few weeks ago. I browsed my inbox and skimmed it again. It was phrased differently, but had same meaning.

Dear Elizabeth,

Nemesis took her revenge, but in an unexpected way. Lately I've been fighting a brave battle with conscience, reason and desire. I admit that I sometimes have made some questionable decisions, and taken stupid risks. But eventually I found out that I am better off listening to my heart and it has chosen Sabine. However, I could still have both Liva and Judy in my life, and in a short period of time, things have worked perfectly fine with all three of them. Just until recently, when Judy told me that she will be leaving.

It has affected me more than I expected. We have so much fun together and I still get warm inside, just by looking at her. As another alcoholic, I can also proudly announce that I have stayed faithful to Sabine for two weeks, so I think it could have worked out fine. But, I will never know now. I have decided that I will not look for a new exotic woman just to keep the model alive. It has been exceptionally nice, and I am grateful that you got me started on the project. In the future I will at least have two three of my women, and that is clearly better than none. And don't worry: I'm sure I can stick to Sabine when it comes to sex.

Love
Christian

I'm not entirely sure, but there is no reason to give Elizabeth cause for yet another reprimand. I am well aware that there may still be situations where I need to think carefully. Suppose Sabine was away for a week and I was sure that only Liva and I was home. Would it not be quite likely that we could agree to keep it secret? From my side it would not even be seen as adultery, but Sabine would probably have a different view if she found out.

So far, the smartest is to not plan anything in full detail, but keep all options open. That strategy has already proved fruitful, and I shall always appreciate a little excitement in everyday life, whether it is just in the world of fantasy. Recently there has been a bit much for my nerves, so it will not hurt to take it a little easy when Judy has left.

All these thoughts are exhausting. I am also getting behind schedule in seeking out new customers, and have once again spent most of the day at the office daydreaming and thinking about women. Normally I would easily be able to switch between a little professional work and a touch of entertainment, but all the implications caused by women are beginning to take the upper hand.

What is most important? Making money or finding true happiness with a partner? It should be possible to combine. The generations before us sure had their own problems, but it was smart in many areas, that one party secured the economic survival, while the other was responsible for the home. As I understand from William' statements from yesterday, it can still be a good model for the few who succeed with it. My years of marriage with Liva was also happy for a long while, so I will not rule out that I might get married again. It is not marriage as an institution, I avoid, but the aggravation and disappointment, if it ends with a break. In a way it seems like a worse defeat when a marriage fails, when we have officially promised each other eternal fidelity, than if you break up with a girlfriend after a few months.

The thought of being married to Sabine attracts me. But to live with both my past and my current wife seems a little absurd. Not exactly illegal, but strange, even to a liberal person like me.

Wednesday 17th November, 2010

In a Better Mood

This morning Benjamin and I tried a new kind of brunch. We had found a place which advertised that you could mix your own instead of getting the traditional dish with everything at once. It is a clever concept because you don't end up having cold pancakes or an entire portion of yogurt left over.

- By the way, you should stop using NanoCover when you clean your motorcycle. I read the other day that it is much more toxic than we are informed about on the packaging.

Aha. So the topic of today was about politically correct cleaning.

- But it works so fine. I hardly need to clean the bike an entire season because the dirt doesn't get stuck.

- Still. It's got something to do with inhaling the particles. They are so tiny that if you compare a nanoparticle with a football, the ratio is the same as between a football and the Earth.

- Haha. In that case, they're real tiny. How can they be toxic?

- I read in an article that mice end up getting damages to their lungs. At least I have stopped using it for my car.

- Hmm. OK, in that case I will consider going back to normal cleaning. What a shame.

It is nice having a friend who keeps abreast of all possible and impossible news. Almost every time I meet Benjamin, he has something new and controversial up his sleeve that he enjoys discussing. Mostly I become wiser, and if I now need a couple of extra hours when I shine my bike, it's a small price to pay for my health. In the winter, I sometimes miss the psychological effect of getting into every corner with a cloth and brush.

As usual with Benjamin we did not address the more tricky topics as love, relationships and everything that I am currently most concerned about, but he noticed that I was a little distracted. I shrugged it off, best as I could and told him that Judy had decided to leave tomorrow. He then suggested that I should find a good gift for her, a sort of souvenir from Denmark that would remind her of the visit in the future.

- Excellent idea, but what should I get her? She travels so lightly and I don't want to bother her with extra baggage. And a t-shirt is ludicrous.

- Hehe. How about a nano-particle wrapped in protective plastic. She'd be able to find room for that.

- Oh come on, now you're annoying. But of course I will think of something. I can go through the Pedestrian Street on the way home, there's a myriad of souvenir shops. And hopefully it isn't just useless junk they have on the shelves.

It turned out after the third shop, that I was on an impossible mission. As Benjamin had said when we arose from the table, I should have thought of it earlier and not be running around in a panic on the last day. But there had been so many other things to deal with in connection with Judy's departure.

A parting gift has a certain symbolic value, and it should preferably not be interpreted incorrectly by Sabine. Perhaps I should also buy something for her? But then she might just think that I have a bad conscience.

When I walked past a goldsmith, I got a sudden impulse. A pair of Marguerite earrings for Judy and something with troll balls for Sabine. This would be appropriate, and I could always postpone giving Sabine her gift until we went to bed. If I noticed that Sabine found it strange when I gave Judy a gift, I could possibly tell her later that it was the purchase of troll balls that had inspired me. Plausible.

Uplifted by my decision I continued my journey home and shopped for our last dinner as a good foursome. A first course of smoked salmon and scrambled eggs on freshly roasted rye bread. That's a nice variant of Judy's new favorite dish - baked grouper with vegetables as the main course and some good cheese with saltcrackers to end it off. That would mean we could get around both champagne, white wine and red wine in a steady flow.

My mood was already much better when I got back. To my own amazement, I had not given it another thought that the time had passed for one last chance of having sex with Judy, and I was quite proud of myself. It was as though I unconsciously, but finally, had realized that she was entering into a new category. The lovely girlfriend, leaving me with priceless memories. Our time together had been short and intense, and we – or I – should just praise my luck. Partly at not being found out and partly at having met the answer to my prayers for the exotic woman in my life. Many things will become easier when she has left, and my irritation will gradually change to a string of good memories.

I was the first to be home, which was also a bit lucky because if Judy had been there in my Jacuzzi again, I would not vouch for my otherwise newfound clarity. No, it was best that I was not exposed to temptation again.

I expect that they will all be home in about an hour, and then we'll have a nice evening with genuine Danish cosiness. The delicate bracelet with troll balls is hidden under Sabine's pillow and I am looking forward to have her unwrap the gift. She usually doesn't wear jewelry, but I hope she likes it.

I owe Benjamin a big thanks for suggesting a gift to Judy. Otherwise, I had probably not realized that Sabine also deserves a physical and lasting evidence of my love. After all, it's not a ring, exaggerating the symbolism, but that opportunity may arise later.

Thursday 18th November, 2010

Self-insight

For the past hour I've been sitting staring at the gift I got
from Judy last night. It gives my office a little personality
and will forever remind me of how special she is. Although
the small glass ball is only a few centimeters tall, it proves
how well she got to know me. It is a mystery to me how she
has found that snowball dolphin, the exact same kind, that
Jacques got from Enzo in the Big Blue movie. It was a good
thing that I had gotten something for her, too.

When we got to the cheese and enjoyed a Chilean Merlot,
Judy fetched three small packages. Xenia got yet another toy
animal for her now sizeable collection and Liva got a fact
book on Argentina. At first I thought that the last one was
for Sabine, but they had perhaps agreed not to endow each
other. So I carefully unpacked the contents, and was very
touched that she remembered my favorite movie when I saw
the snowball.

- You don't have that in your collection, do you?

- Haha. And you even remember the quote from the scene.
Good job, Judy! Incidentally, I also have a little something
for you, so you remember Denmark.

As soon as she unwrapped her gift, she exchanged her gold
earrings with the delicate, small marguerite flowers. They
suited her excellently, and she smiled brightly. Intoxicated
by the sight and the previous glasses of wine, I was just
about to make a speech, but contented himself by telling the

girls that I loved them all. Each in a distinct way, and there was no competition, they just made me so happy to be alive.

We decided to watch the Big Blue again after we had cleaned up in the kitchen. When I later hit the sack with Sabine, she found her own gift, where I had placed it under her pillow. She was a bit embarrassed, but I could see that she was happy with my gesture. I managed to refrain from any explanation of which purchase had inspired the other by giving in to my urge of kissing instead of talking.

This morning we ordered a big taxi and all went to the Central Station and found the correct platform, where Judy was to embark on her trip through Europe. We hugged for a long time and told her to send us some beautiful postcards. I helped her carry the luggage into the train, and when I gave her one last hug, she said that perhaps we just might have time for a quickie in the toilet. Immediately I got a flashback from the Glyptotek, and she secured herself another imprint in my memory. She also said that maybe we could meet in some dreams to come. I could not suppress a silly laugh when leaving the train.

When the train had departed, Liva said that she had an appointment in town, and Sabine needed to visit the Royal Library for some special books, so I wandered off to my office alone. It feels like a very special era is over and I cannot understand it is only a little over a month ago, I saw Judy for the first time. She will always be in my thoughts, and it will take some time before I fall completely to rest by her absence.

"Vaya Con Dios" I wrote in a text message to her when I put the dolphin on my desk and she has just replied with the most brief, but perhaps best message I ever received: "Kys". That was one of her favorite words from the Danish language.

My next thought is that I might get bored. But nothing suggests that Sabine will become tedious, and with the prospect of following Xenia's upbringing at close quarters, I also get an insight into the joys of being a sort of reserve parent. But she needs to be couple of years older, before I take huge interest. By then some of the dolls and stuffed animals also need to be replaced with a racetrack. I have noticed that Sabine gets that unique expression in her eyes when she sits with a baby in her arms. So far, she hasn't started talking about having children, and in my eyes it's smartest to wait until she has finished her studies. But then she will be out to find a job. If we continue to think like that, it will never be the right time to have kids. As long as we have Xenia with us, however, my needs in those areas are covered well.

It is quite incredible so much havoc Elizabeth's mail, nearly three months ago, has created in my life. Here I am, thinking about having children, where I previously would swear that it was nothing for me. When I see my friends with children of many different age groups, I am happy with my choice, but having both Sabine and Xenia at such close quarters has apparently affected my attitude. I ought to have a chat with Sabine soon about our future, whether it be short or long term.

When I think back on the last few months, I don't recognize myself. If my first conversation with Liva had not brought such fond memories about the good time we had together, I would under no circumstances have prompted Sabine to move in with me. The decision was taken without my normal need to think deeply. Virtually all of my experience tells me that it makes sense to wait a bit, and I acted blinded by my infatuation. I should have known better.

If Liva had asked to stay with me before Sabine had moved in, I would not have come to this situation, so quickly, either. In that case, I would have helped Liva and held Sabine on the sidelines for a while. Who knows, some months, maybe. That would have suited me better, I'm sure. Moreover, I would hardly have run into Judy, but what good is all of this analysis when things have already happened?

I cannot very well throw out Liva and Sabine now. But I can take myself seriously and learn from my self-insight. When Judy left, I was unprepared, and now I realize that Liva at some point will move on in her life, too. Until then I will get the best out of living with her and Sabine. Learn a little more about the implications of having a small child in one's life. Take more notice on how my love for Sabine evolves, and last but not least start to listen a little more to myself.

I must respect myself to gain respect from others. Likewise, the women in my life need to take me as I am.

Friday the 19th November, 2010

A New Plan Emerges

Sabine and Liva have both gone to bed, each with a book. Xenia was put to sleep many hours ago and I once more sit pondering the small and large changes, life has come to the habit of bringing me lately.

Just as I had concluded that a life with my ex-wife, her child and maybe my coming wife had its advantages, the situation changed again. Liva was about to feed Xenia when I came into the kitchen. I began to cook adult food for the rest of us because Sabine had sent me an SMS that she was on her way home from the library. It warmed me to look forward to a peaceful evening.

Following Judy's exit it was a little easier to mix subjects, to talk all at once and generally just babble away about this and that. It had not dawned on me until now that the presence of a foreigner, despite her excellent command of our language had affected our conversations when we were all together. Maybe it played a part that she was always a center of attention, not least from my side, so without her – a new situation. Last night was the first time I had found myself with peace of mind in the strange mix of well-known comfort mixed with a perfect touch of freshness. It was like trying a new meal with unexpected spices. We could talk about everything, and talked about our different experiences with Judy. I could feel that she had left her marks all the way around.

- I will never forget how all the guys at our party tried to hide their fascination for her. It was like candid camera, said

Liva, and was amused by my friends' behavior. I saw no reason to defend them, for it had indeed been evident.

- Well, no wonder. She can get any guy to look twice. As far as I know, it didn't come to more, so I think she leaves Denmark as an excellent ambassador for Argentina.

- That was only because none of them were men enough to invite her out on the dance floor when we went over to the Park Café.

Apparently Sabine had also observed that Judy ended up bored in their company. I was a little nervous about whether our conversation would evolve into the consequences of Judy leaving the party, but fortunately Sabine and Liva just continued talking about in the evening at the Park.

Back to the new situation. Liva said she had been wondering if she should get back to Mick for a long time. Her staying here in my apartment had helped. The input she had received from both Sabine and Judy had mostly passed over my head, but had evidently influenced her decision.

We all knew that Liva's job was influenced by the aftermath of the global economic crisis. Each month, they had said goodbye to good colleagues. To avoid ending up in the depths of useless job offers from her union, Liva had then reached out in her network and landed a new job in Aarhus. I choked on a mouthful of the lasagne, when she told us. It surprised me that she had acted so promptly.

- Aarhus? Are you moving to Aarhus?

- Yes, I am. And I have some spare vacation, so it's happening already this coming weekend. My current contract allows me to terminate with immediate effect and I have been promised a company-paid apartment over there until I find my own.

- But what about Mick? Have you completely dropped a future with him? Sabine asked.

Liva said that during the past month she had concluded that she did not need the comfort of a traditional family. Especially not with a man whom she almost never saw.

- Well, cheers then. I'm surprised, but happy on your behalf. You will probably make a good difference in the new company, but you will be missed here.

- Thank you. It won't hurt the two of you to get a little more time alone. Are you aware of how strange it has been to live here? Not to mention the bizarre situation when Judy was here too? I have never experienced anything like it.

Sabine and I quickly agreed that we also considered the last month as a most peculiar experience, but just as quickly that we had learned a lot and would not have been without a single moment. Exactly what experience, Sabine has built, I am not aware, but I was happy to hear her agreement. She has spent many hours in the living room with Liva and Judy where I was not involved. For all I know, they could have talked about Sex and the City or what it was like to have sex with me. They had all three surprised me before, but I hoped that it was Carrie and her friends they'd been talking about if I really had to choose.

Everything about decisions and being in control of my own life ends up being nothing but a hypothetical situation. I have lost Judy as my exotic woman. Now I lose Liva as my soul mate. Sabine might turn out to be my new lifelong partner, but I'd better wait and see. Buying gifts to Sabine time and again to prove my love is not a long lasting solution. We have not even had time to get to know each other quietly, as I prefer, because our lives have been filled with the extra company. If I want to avoid losing her too, I better think carefully.

Deep down, I am very aware of what I want, but taught by the impulsive action earlier, it is smartest to take another breath before I follow my intuition about the best way to secure my future with Sabine.

Fortunately, she is right in there, ready to be sent into even better dreams, and I would be a darn fool if I did not use the opportunity to examine exactly how well I know her. I wonder if she will agree to be awakened before she reaches her full, deep sleep? Of course she will.

Monday 22nd November, 2010

New Thoughts

The Central Station is starting to cause me trauma. Yesterday we sent Liva and Xenia off to Aarhus, and once again there was hugging on the platform. We joked a little that she should send us a postcard, or at least send us some pictures of the temporary apartment in an email.

Their baggage consisted of only a few suitcases, so it did not seem as a proper moving out, but she had arranged with Mick to have some furniture sent later. It might easily take her a couple of months to find a more permanent place. Her room at my place is back to the original function as a combined storage and wasted space.

We had spent the entire Saturdays cleaning. I think it worked as a sort of psychological hygiene for all of us. The mood was only slightly depressed, but as the hours passed and we could see how the joint effort was successful, we cheered up.

- Look at the positive side, now you have the entire place to yourselves.

- Yeah right, I do not use half the space in my apartment. It was so perfect that both Judy and you were here.

Sabine was a bit quiet and I was briefly worried whether she felt inadequate.

- I miss Judy, too, but it is easier to concentrate on my studies when I'm not tempted to sit and talk every night.

We did, however, talk all Saturday evening, and we completely forgot to turn on the television. After having dinner, we were sitting in the kitchen and talked about Liva's new job. She had found out that a former colleague had started by himself in Aarhus and had built a healthy business. Previously, they had worked really well together and she looked forward to the new challenges – not least escaping the bad situation in the old job.

- Oh, I hope the labor market looks better when I'm done studying.

- It'll be a few years from now, right? A lot can change. Just look at how much change we've had here in such a short time.

- He is right, Sabine. Just focus on learning as much as possible and start building a network. The vast majority of jobs are never posted but found through friends and contacts.

Here we were, acting as parents to Sabine giving good advice about the future. It seemed comical and comforting at the same time. She could almost be our daughter, but I did not get the feeling that she felt inferior. It was probably thanks to all the previous conversations with Liva that she was accustomed to listen to her experiences. Once again, I was curious about what they might have discussed during the long hours that I had not attended. It was inappropriate to ask about it, so I had to live with my uncertainty and just be glad they had become such good friends.

Sabine and I went for a long walk after we had said goodbye to Liva and Xenia. We had considered taking a train out to

Klampenborg and walk around in the park but ended up strolling around the city. When we got a little cold, we sat at a café and looked through the weekend newspapers. We did not talk much, but probably both thought about all the experiences we've been through.

I think we shared the feeling of wanting to postpone our return to an empty apartment. Sabine had virtually been surrounded by lively discussions and a guarantee of sociability since she moved in. She had indeed moved from her rented room without knowing how big the contrast would be, but it was clear that she had enjoyed having Judy and Liva stay with us. To me, the change had been equally big. There is a difference between living as an adult family with many members and to just being two. When I was married to Liva, it was ultimately my dilemma that I really would rather live alone than be stuck in a relationship where there was nothing new. My chance with Sabine is that she is usually in a dynamic environment and can help me with a breath of fresh input. It has already been exciting to follow her reports, and I have been watching a few movies, I hadn't thought would interest me.

After we had plowed through the last newspapers after the third stop for coffee, I could feel Sabine looking at me.

- I know you miss them, but let's go home now. I'll cook a delicious dinner, and then I have a movie you'll like from the university.

- Yes. Apologies for being so quiet. It is impolite of me to be so withdrawn and I would very much like to go home. As Liva said at one point, there are some advantages to having the entire place to ourselves.

It hadn't just been thoughts about Liva's and Judy's absence that had occupied me.

She smiled and said that it was not that kind of a movie, she wanted to show me. Sometimes it doesn't take much to lift my spirits. A smile and an allusion can do wonders, and we left the last café in a better mood than when we arrived.

Later

Right now a wonderful scent is emanating from the kitchen, and Sabine has been busy out there for more than an hour. She insisted that I should not help, but she has repeatedly been passing by to pour wine into my glass. Each time, accompanied by warm kisses and assurances that everything is going fine in the kitchen. She is really doing an effort. In a way, I prefer that we help each other, but I'm doing my best to enjoy her service. I can always retaliate later. After all, it is easier for me now to focus when there is only her to seduce. Or to be seduced by. I have a feeling that she wants to prove her worth, and that is not necessary at all.

Tuesday 23rd November, 2010

The Decision

Dear Christian and Sabine,

The trip to Aarhus went smoothly. Xenia slept most of the way, and I had time to study the many magazines you had bought for me. Thank you for your good company during the time I have been living with you. It has given me much needed input, and it feels absolutely right to have moved on now. As you can see from the pictures, I ended up in a somewhat smaller place, but that makes cleaning easier. It's nice here and I am sure that Aarhus can be a good base for me and Xenia.

Take care of each other and avoid getting lost in life or the big apartment.

Hugs from Liva

Her place looked really small from the pictures, but she did not need much space. As far as I could see, there was only one room and one bedroom, and both were already strewn with toys. The furniture looked old, and I thought that she might miss her own stuff. While she lived with us, she commented several times how funny it was to find herself among such a well-known interior. She had been there back when most of the furniture was purchased all those years ago. It will be good for her to start over, and if her salary turns out to be good enough, I think that she drops having Mick send over her part of the furniture from their home.

She has changed a lot since we were married. Perhaps we both have, and I remember the good talk we had about my conscience regarding Sabine at the beginning of this month. Liva had been so sympathetic and gave me good advice when she could in principle have scolded me for my behavior. At the same time we were both to blame on one cause of my frustrations, so her reaction was possibly a form of justification to herself. If she could forgive me on Sabine's behalf, or at least defuse my problems, her own guilt also diminished. I imagine that I myself would act similarly in such a situation, although it is difficult to put myself in exactly her place.

This line of thought further had me recall Judy's advice the day after my talk with Liva. It was characteristic for each of them that Liva had talked about creating security for Sabine and myself while Judy had been more into the somewhat mysterious. I never got around to tell Judy about that night when I managed to weave my dreams into Sabine's, and strangely enough, Sabine and I haven't talked about it, either. There has been too much going on, but at some point I have to try it again.

My only attempt to get some response to the weird dream was when I brought it up with Nikolai. I had hoped that my retelling could bring some clarity, but he had been rather uninterested. It may be that the reports of other peoples' dreams are like watching their vacation pictures. You needed to have been there to really see the significance. Or you needed to be more curious. Marie would probably have been good at commenting, but it was too cumbersome to explain in an email. All the same, it had been a good therapy to write her more regularly and she will be getting an update again soon. But I'd rather wait until Sabine and I have found our new rhythm after Judy and Liva moved out.

That must be how it feels when your children grow up and leave home. Ulrich had given me some good prospects in that direction when he compared my love for three women to his love for his kids. It was different in many areas, and he does not lose his children when they move away from home. He can get used to the idea over a period of several years and I have in just a few months gone through the entire spectrum of the transition from being single to almost bigamist and am now in an ordinary relationship.

Maybe it's not too late to build the same joy with Sabine, as William said was of such importance in his life. The part about getting home to his family, but he had his children at a good time. After hearing so much from Nikolai about the sleepless nights, I am not prepared to duplicate his feat. If we could adopt a trouble free teenager, it would be much easier. But that concept is probably a contradiction, no matter how good upbringing they have received. And if they come from a healthy home, why would they be given up for adoption?

When Daniel and Mikkel cheered me up after the news that I missed Judy, I was reassured by the understanding that good friends can be a healthy substitute for the social life, one establishes with a family. Again I must remind myself that I should be grateful for what I have.

My biggest risk in the near future is that Sabine has yet to establish close friendships. I can get a little nervous that she relies too much on our mutual company, because that's exactly where can I see a pattern that I dislike. Until now she has been as preoccupied as I with our experiences with Judy and Liva, so I understand if she hasn't bonded more with her fellow students, but it would be best if she gets some new friends. I find great pleasure in meeting with my various friends spread evenly over a month. If I start to cancel my social life, I know myself well enough to realize I'll get ratty. But I also think it is too sad for Sabine if she is left to herself a few times or more every week. Until now, I could get out knowing that the three girls were company for each other, but now she could feel alone in the unpleasant way because, after all, this is not her own home. Not least, the memories of the many girly nights must be firmly planted in her consciousness, and that kind of sociability does not come back.

This is why I suppress my desire for a spontaneous evening beer and decide to get home from the office in time to be there before Sabine. Her dinner last night was sufficient enough for us to heat the remains tonight, and there is no reason to reciprocate with another huge effort into the culinary area.

On the way home I will visit a flower shop and make sure that there are fresh bouquets in both the kitchen and living room. It could also be an idea to repeat my success from her first night and persuade her to an evening bath with a scent of roses. She deserves to be pampered, and I want to be the one doing it.

There is something symbolic in returning to our original starting where things were less complicated than they eventually became. If I had known then what the next months meant, I'm not sure I would have gotten up the next morning.

Maybe I can persuade Sabine to stay at home in bed tomorrow.

Wednesday 24th November, 2010

Honesty

My theory proved correct. It is a great idea to think carefully when it comes to new plans. Maybe it's just me, but I think men in general can take a little longer dealing with feelings than women. It wasn't until after I had received input from my various friends and spent time analyzing myself in depth, that I was ready to react on my conclusion.

My plan was to convey the news to Sabine as honestly and gently as possible. She came home to a fragrant apartment with me waiting in the sofa with an appetizer and a bottle of the same red wine that we had on our first date at the MASH restaurant. A nice Chilean red, going well with humus on salted crackers. When she dropped her bag on the floor and sat down in the sofa, I was sure it would become a good evening.

- Cheers and welcome home. How was your day at the university?

- Oh, well. A little slow I think. We've had three lectures, and there wasn't much new in substance. Analyzing the symbolism in commercials. It can sometimes seem a little like high school, where the obvious becomes too elevated.

She should go out and find a meaningful job in my opinion. It has always been my position that you learn more doing business than in school, but I've also been fortunate in being able to jump from one career and specialty to the next without the need for exam papers.

- Stay with it, dear. Just be glad that it sometimes comes easily to you. Alternatively, you need to take a different angle and find a job where the challenges may give you an even better experience than studying.

- That's easy for you to say. I can be in doubt about the future sometimes, but as far as my studying, I will stick to it. It is important for me to get a proof of my knowledge.

In doubt? About the future? Maybe she had been thinking that we proceeded to quickly with our relationship as well, but I chose to not pay more attention to that possibility.

- Tonight you should just relax. I'm going to heat the remains from your lovely dinner yesterday, and there is more of the good wine.

It was not in order to calm my nerves or get her drunk, but I wanted to ensure that the atmosphere was relaxed. With a good meal in a cozy environment, I could show Sabine how I also wanted to service her and be there if she had had a bad day. It was important for me to lay a positive foundation before I came to the more serious part of my plan.

When doing the dishes, I thought it was a good time to air my thoughts about our future.

- There is something we need to talk about.

- Hmm. That sounds serious.

- Well, I think my decision is to the best for both of us in the long term.

- Ehm, what have you decided?

- You know that I was originally looking for three women and in an unexpected way, and not least very quickly, both you, Judy and Liva became a part of my life. This has given me cause for much contemplation.

- I'd better open another bottle, while you tell me what you have decided.

There was no way to sweeten it. I started to tell her about the deep impression she had made from the very first time we met. She had caused me to doubt whether I should continue looking for my two other women, but also been instrumental that one by one they showed up. During the time we all lived together, I had opportunities to assess where I really wanted to go with my project. Without getting into all my temptations, I explained that it had soon dawned on me that she was more than an infatuation. I wanted her more than I had expected.

Precisely because Liva and Judy so beautifully represented the other two women I had looked for, it was possible for me to consider the new model with extra care. It remains my point that one cannot expect one partner to meet all your needs, but my feelings for Sabine and my conscience was not to be ignored. I had to take it seriously when it was she who filled my thoughts time and time again. Had it not been for Liva and Judy and I had continued to go on dates, I would hardly have reached the same conclusion. At least not in such a short time, because in that case I would not have asked Sabine to move in so quickly.

She let me speak at length without interrupting.

- ... So to make a long story meaningful, I propose that we start from scratch in a way. This is why I have made sure that we can continue this evening as we did the first time you visited here. Would you like a bath?

She sat there quietly for a while, but it was a big mouthful. I went to fill my Jacuzzi and thought this would make or break. With the risk that she was disappointed or even angry, it was still best to speak out clearly on my part. I prefer to be open and honest and know that I'm faithful to my own beliefs. She entered the bathroom just as the tub was filled.

- When you said we had to start over, did you refer to more than just pretend this evening was our first?

- Yes. There is more to it. I love you so much that I do not want to risk getting tired of you. While this may sound like a paradox, it is best that you move back to your rented room. We have a much greater chance of a future together, if we proceed more cautiously. Believe me, I know myself well enough to be sure about this.

She started to undress carefully, and I could feel I had done the right thing – in being honest to us both.

Thursday 25th November, 2010

Control

Dear Elizabeth,

I hope you have time to come by for a chat tomorrow evening. I'll arrange for dinner, but mostly I need to talk some things over. On Saturday Liva moved to Aarhus, she has found a new job over there. Today Sabine moved back to her rented room on my request, but in shared understanding.

As I have told you during the course of the last few months, it has been something of a roller coaster ride with ups and downs. Now I cannot figure out whether I have acted incorrectly and would like to hear your opinion. But it is not suitable for emails, I think. Come by at seven o'clock and cancel any other appointments, please.

Love

Christian

It was the shortest summary I could give her, but enough for her to prepare for a good talk. She has recently been through the whole emotional register with all her men, and I've been too preoccupied with my own challenges to hear more about her progress.

Perhaps it's a strange solution I have come to, but I have not pushed away Sabine, rather the contrary. I'm curious to hear if Elizabeth understands my action and what she has to say.

If anyone can put themself in my situation, it must be her. Many of my friends will probably think I have lost my mind, but they have not gone through this exercise of giving relationships the serious consideration that we have. Our ways to implement it have been different, but our motives are alike.

Friday 26th November, 2010

What Have I Learned?

One of my favorite scenes from the world of movies is when Sue asks Crocodile Dundee, whether they have psychologists out at Walkabout Creek. He answers that if you have problems, you just tell Wally and the day after everybody knows about it. Problem over. That is perhaps a bit like bartenders for men and hairdressers for women in our part of the world, except that they preferably shouldn't pass the story on. In the absence of my own Wally and instead of entrusting myself to a bartender, it is good to know Elizabeth.

She arrived a few minutes past seven, and we sat down in the living room with a couple of dry martinis before dinner. I gave her the longer story about everything that had happened since Liva moved last weekend. She listened to my memories of both Judy and Liva.

- What do you think about all of this yourself? What have you learned?

- At first I was quite confused, but recently everything fell into place. It is true that I need time by myself. I need to long for Sabine, too. Do you remember the song about 'Love is a matter of distanceĒ? There is something to that.

- I'm not sure you grasped the meaning of the song, but fair enough. I understand what you mean. But you did not answer my questions.

- Oh, right. What I think and what I've learned? Hmm. I think that I've been incredibly lucky. You got me pulled out of a long period of too much focus on my professional life and a boring celibacy. I think it has been extremely entertaining and occasionally almost too exciting. But I have also learned that I have limits...

- What do you mean, limits?

As another psychologist Elizabeth was eminent at asking questions and provoking me to contemplate my feelings.

- Well, as an example, there's Karla, whom I met on a date. She turned out to be married, and I could not accept initiating a relationship with her. In hindsight that wasn't the sole reason, because she also blatantly lied to her husband, while I overheard their conversation. I need to trust a woman. I want to be honest and ask the same back. How would I ever be able to believe in what she said?

- Aha. Fidelity is important to you. But if you start having relationships with several women at the same time, are you faithful to them all, then?

- You see, this is another area I have learned something about. After a short time I became aware that my conscience overshadowed the desire to continue with Judy and Liva. You know me well enough to know I'm not jumping just any girl. Some of my friends fit better to the myth about us men in that regard. I need to feel an extra dimension, and was fulfilled by all three of them at first. In three different ways and that is also why they fit so perfectly into my model. But I could not complete it at the end.

- Does that bother you?

- No, not really. I am happy to say I have some integrity. And frankly, it could have ended so horribly wrong.

- What are you going to do now?

- I will lead you to my kitchen and stand by my promise about dinner.

Throughout dinner we talked more about how our generation enters into relationships with new and different presumptions. It seemed like an inexhaustible topic. Her attempt to be with three men over a prolonged period of time had, as my own with three women, gone fine for a while. But as you can almost predict, her handyman started to expect a little more reward than dinner. Is it really sex destroying so much? According to Maslow, sex ranks right after feeling safe and secure when we go to sleep without being hungry. But then again, his pyramid of needs is from 1943, and Elizabeth and I agreed that times have changed since then. Especially with regard to household structures.

As she brought to my attention, I also still have Sabine in my life, albeit under new circumstances. She reassured me and thought it was for my own good. My conversation with Liva at the French Café had inspired me to relive the close relationship I'd had with her, but I had acted a little hastily when I had so spontaneously asked Sabine to move in with me.

I was simply so moved by my feelings that I forgot everything else. And like Elizabeth said at one point, she can at times feel like she's seventeen inside, so she knows what I mean.

What started out as a fun experiment has given me a number of experiences I will never forget. All worked out pretty well despite some intense challenges, and now I have Sabine. She agrees that we shouldn't be in such a hurry and I am grateful that she understands me. She said she knew about that part of me, because her many conversations with Liva had given her more insight into how I gradually felt myself trapped in marriage. With or without those official documents in a relationship, the same can easily happen to me again if I do not take my own experience seriously.

It certainly helps that Sabine is young enough to not want to build a home in the same manner as a woman who focuses on forming a family. In that way, I am extra lucky because I will probably never want that. I have completely suspended my thoughts about one day being married to Sabine and will just enjoy our time together as long as possible. She still has the key to my apartment, and we agree that the winter weekends will probably be spent being together here. In this way, I can also continue my weekly social life without feeling trapped at home.

Best of all is the feeling that it is no longer women who control my life. That has been the case before, and especially in the last couple of months, until it finally dawned on me that I needed to listen to myself and act in accordance with my own feelings, even if it means making my woman unhappy. That way I can meet her with respect and she can consider my offer better.